The Heist

Also from C. W. Gortner

The First Actress
The Romanov Empress
Marlene
The Vatican Princess
Mademoiselle Chanel
The Queen's Vow
The Confessions of Catherine De Medici
The Last Queen
The Tudor Secret
The Tudor Conspiracy
The Tudor Vendetta

C. W. Gortner and M.J. Rose
The Steal
The Bait
The Heist

Also from M.J. Rose

The Last Tiara
Cartier's Hope
Tiffany Blues
The Library of Light and Shadow
The Secret Language of Stones
The Witch of Painted Sorrows
The Collector of Dying Breaths
The Seduction of Victor H.
The Book of Lost Fragrances
The Hypnotist
The Memoirist
The Reincarnationist
Lip Service
In Fidelity
Flesh Tones
Sheet Music
The Halo Effect
The Delilah Complex
The Venus Fix
Lying in Bed

M.J. Rose and Steve Berry
The Museum of Mysteries
The Lake of Learning
The House of Long Ago
The End of Forever

M.J. Rose and C. W. Gortner
The Steal
The Bait
The Heist

M.J. Rose and Randy Susan Meyers
The Fashion Orphans

The Heist

C.W. GORTNER

and

M.J. ROSE

BLUE
BOX
PRESS

The Heist
By C. W. Gortner and M.J. Rose

Copyright 2022 C. W. Gortner and M.J. Rose
ISBN: 978-1-952457-91-3

Published by Blue Box Press, an imprint of Evil Eye Concepts, Incorporated

1959

There comes a time in life when a man has to admit he has no choice but to cut his losses. I've rarely encountered those times, and I'd like to say that when I have, I've been strong enough to admit it. But it hasn't happened very often; it's been a source of pride that no matter what life throws at me, I can handle it. Maybe not in the most delicate way, but hey, I'm not a butler. I'm a soldier. The Army trained me to assess a situation, to figure out how much risk it posed to my safety, and then decide how to efficiently reduce my risk and get the job done.

During the war, I traveled from the chaos of Rome to the sinister grimness of Paris and then through bomb-shattered Germany to the rubble of Berlin. I saw things that few others had, things that still haunt me—and I hunted down the monsters who let it all happen. It wasn't an easy job, and it wasn't a pretty one. I made one mistake that I regret. Later on, as an insurance investigator for Lambert Securities, I had to use those same skills to survey a crime scene, figure out who might have stolen the loot and how they did it, and then determine how to get the loot back before the client filed a claim that would cost my employer millions. It wasn't an easy job, either, but I can truthfully say that I never made a mistake. The rules for hunting down escaped Nazis are the same as those for catching a thief: assess the risk to your personal safety, the likelihood of surviving the mission, and any weaknesses that might give you or your opponent an advantage.

It's not pretty, but it's simple.

That is until I got involved with Ania Thorne. And you see, that's when the rules went out the window. She glided into my life with those gorgeous cat eyes and ballet dancer legs and turned me inside out. Everything went by the wayside. Or, if I'm totally honest, I threw them out the window. Because once I had her in my arms, there was no going back to rules. She was playing dirty for keeps, and rules weren't her style. It surprised me—and it had been a very long time since anyone had surprised me—and it thrilled me. It also scared the hell out of me. She was way out of my league, and I fell hard. Before I even knew it, I was in over my head. Now, it bears asking: How does a guy who hunted war criminals and investigated high-profile thefts get in over his head with a woman?

Well, Ania isn't just any woman. She's a soldier, too—only one who designs very expensive jewelry for a living and has a lot more disposable cash. To catch a leopard, she knew how to bait her trap. When it sprang on us instead, she assessed the risks to our personal safety, the likelihood of survival, and any weaknesses that might give her or our opponent an advantage.

Turned out, I was both the risk and her weakness. So, like any well-trained soldier, she cut her losses. Those decisions had to be made to increase the likelihood of survival.

The strangest part is, I get it. I really do. I get why she ditched me. She is way out of my league and has diamond dust in her veins. Like every soldier does, she understands that there comes a time when the mission has to come first.

I really do get it. That doesn't mean it's pretty or that it makes it any easier.

Because I can't seem to do the same thing with her.

Chapter One

Jerome

London in the winter stinks. It's cold and damp, and it rains like it's never rained before. Which, in England, is pretty much biblical, no matter the season. So why December has to dial it up to an apocalyptic level beats the hell out of me. When the temperature gets low enough and it starts to snow, that's the icing on the shit sundae. Slush and mud-splash and days so short you're waking up in the dark and leaving work in the dark. You never see the sun. And, yeah, it's England, so the sun only makes guest appearances, but from December to May…forget it. You'd better really like Christmas because it's the only thing that's getting you through the end of the year to spring.

Not too long ago, I wouldn't have cared. Rainy weather never bothered me. Crappy pub food and mud on my shoes never put a dent in my fender.

Ania changed all that. After five-star hotels and gourmet meals—even if I never understood why anyone needs more than one fork to eat their dinner—greasy fish and chips, and London's famous red double-deckers spraying snow-slush all over me no longer have the same charm.

Three days before Christmas Eve, I leave my latest dead-end job standing guard at a third-tier jewelry shop, feeling like I have the snow-slush running in my veins.

"Have a lovely Christmas, Mr. Curtis," calls the pretty blond secretary, whose name I never remember. It forces me to smile and say,

"Yeah, you, too." She's been trying for weeks to get me to take her out, not openly but in that tight-skirt-and-bend-suggestively-over-the teapot kind of way. The jeweler is closed for the holiday. He's made his profit selling low-end watches, necklaces, bracelets, and rings that would make Ania grimace at the shoddy craftsmanship and has a family to celebrate with. His secretary is single, like me, and desperate to remedy that.

I'm desperate to keep it that way.

Reaching my flat in Earl's Court involves either the smelly Tube or a crowded, sauna-like bus ride. I decide to hop the Tube to avoid arriving in my flat covered in double-decker road splash, not that anything but a very dead plant and a bottle of whiskey is waiting for me there. I stand, gripping the overhead rail as flustered last-minute Christmas shoppers shove their way in with enough Harrods gift bags to bring joy to an orphanage. Everyone looks out of sorts and on the verge of panic in the lead-up to the big event of Christmas Day. The jabbing of elbows and utterances of "Pardon me, chap" as they fill the carriage with their packages—a few with the befuddled look of belated realization regarding how much they've overspent—rubs my nerves raw.

I need a drink. And a cigarette. And greasy fish and chips.

That's going to be my Christmas extravaganza.

As I trudge out of the station toward my flat, Earl's Court sparkles with Christmas lights, and people are either scrambling to get home with their armfuls of packages or going into the local pubs to drown their over-budget sorrows. I'd been hoping to maybe indulge my lead-up to the big event at the pub myself, but one look inside at the smoke-choked, clamoring mob, and I turn on my heel. Buying my fish and chips at a local stall, I begin eating out of the oily bag as I walk up the street to the nondescript post-war building and single-room apartment I call home.

I smell the cigarette smoke before I hear the voice. The smoke is sharp in the frigid air and has a distinct American tang to it, as does the voice.

"That stuff will kill you, you know. It's batter and grease deep-fried over batter and grease."

She's leaning against my building, her cigarette tip glowing as she takes an inhale. For a paralyzing second, through some trick of the flickering streetlamp, I think it's Ania, and my entire body goes numb. Then I blink. Ania never smokes, and she hated it when I did. And then the woman says, "Well? Is this any way to say hi to an old friend who's been freezing her tuchus off waiting for you?"

Lauren Segal. The seafoam eyes that are always a little too direct. The mop of reddish curls, only tonight they're groomed in a svelte swoop under her scarf. Pert nose with a smattering of freckles. Pert lips, too, very red. She always goes a little overboard on the lipstick when she uses it.

"Oh, hey." I jolt toward her, feeling like a jerk for my lack of enthusiasm.

She grinds out her cigarette and gives me a smile. "Surprised to see me?"

"I am." I force a return smile, and it feels all wrong on my face, like I've forgotten how. "I thought you weren't coming back here until the new year. Or did I…?"

I fumble for my keys as she says, "No, you didn't forget. I was supposed to come in February to set up advance press for *The Treasure of Kilimanjaro*, but we delayed the London premiere. I have a boatload of meetings instead, so I thought I'd hop over the pond early and see my favorite stranger." She takes my food from me so I can unlock the building's door. "And here you are, eating your heart attack. And, really, Jerome, looking very down in the mouth."

"It's Christmas," I reply, now fiddling with the key to my flat door, which is never amenable to letting me in without a struggle. "Isn't being down in the mouth sort of required?"

"I wouldn't know. I'm Jewish. We celebrate Hanukkah."

"Huh, right. So, not down in the mouth?" I push open my door and step aside to let her in, then flip on the overhead lamp. The sink is piled with dishes, though I really should eat my heart attack on a plate since Lauren is here. Try to look as if I have some interest in being civilized. I'm relieved as I take a quick look around—my flat is so small that one look is all that's required—to see that I managed to throw my dirty socks and shorts into the bathroom hamper before I left for work this morning. I had been hungover, so I wasn't sure. My bed pulls out of the sofa, and a piece of the sheet and blanket are dangling on the floor.

"Well, it's eight days of holiday for us, so there's plenty of guilt to go around to compensate for the down-in-the-mouth." Lauren laughs, taking off her coat. Her laughter catches me off guard. It's spontaneous and warm—like she is. "Jerome. Eat your dinner out of the bag. I don't care."

I chuckle and point to the table by my bed-slash-sofa. "There's a bottle of scotch and what I think is a clean glass."

"Great. I need it." She pours herself a drink while I hastily wash a plate for myself, dump my soggy fish and chips onto it, and join her on the couch. She's sitting with her legs crossed in slacks, her glass in hand. It strikes me that she's come to see me in London four times now in the past year, always on business for her father's movie studio, and has never once expected me to ask her out to dinner. Nor has she bent over suggestively to offer me a look at her tuchus.

She's like an old war buddy, which is strange because we don't really know each other that well. She helped me out of that jam in Venice and left for Los Angeles the very next day, unaware until several months later when she tracked me down in London that my entire world had been shattered. Since then, she's made a point of sending a telegram every time she's going to be in town, and I never remember the exact day until she appears on my doorstep.

Another girl, one like Ania, would just cut her losses. But Lauren never seems to mind that I've become what polite society would term a non-starter. Or where I come from, a loser. She keeps visiting me and not expecting anything but conversation and good scotch. And even though I'm a mess, I'm not blind. I know she must like me as more than a war buddy, but she's not pushing it.

"Any plans for the holiday?" she asks, lighting a cigarette and passing me the pack after I finish my meal.

"Nope." I resist a burp and take one of her Lucky Strikes. "Just going to stay home and pretend it's not happening until it's time to ring in 1960. A new decade and all that."

She smiles over her cigarette. "And maybe a new start? Because I have a present for you."

Oh, no.

"You really shouldn't have." I cough, scattering ash over myself. I use the uncomfortable moment to get up and fetch another ashtray. "I don't do Christmas."

"Neither do I, remember? It's not a Christmas present. It's a job offer."

"What?" I stand with the extra ashtray in my hand in the middle of my living room-slash-bedroom and think I must look as baffled as I feel.

"Before you say no—" She motions for me to sit back down. "Just hear me out. It's a good job that'll make use of your skills. It pays pretty well, too. No, wait. Listen to me first." Her tone isn't punitive. It's direct, like her eyes. It's one of the things I respect about her. She doesn't beat around the bush. She's like California: What you see is what you get. "You're not happy here. You're not doing anything you enjoy—"

"Hey. I like standing guard over cheap watches," I say, pouring her another glass.

"You don't. And you won't even be standing guard over cheap watches by the time we ring in the new decade. You'll leave like you have from every other job since you came back to London. You don't want things to be permanent. No commitment," she says, "means no disappointment."

I don't answer, blowing smoke toward the ceiling and feeling that snow-sludge in my veins.

"Aren't you going to ask me what the job is?" she says.

"Sure, I'll bite." I return my gaze to her. "What's the job?"

"Security chief for my father's studio."

Now, I must really look like an idiot. I feel my mouth hanging open. "Are you serious?"

"As serious as that heart-attack dinner of yours." Her voice turns brisk, the studio head's daughter driving home the deal. "We need someone to oversee our security. The reason we decided to delay our London premiere is because we've gotten advance word through the grapevine that our movie is going to be nominated for an Academy Award, and so is our lead actress for her role in it. Eva Elain is about to become an even bigger star and pain in the ass than she already is. We're up against heavy competition from MGM's *Ben Hur*, so we're planning a big pre-Oscar rollout. It's our first nominated picture, and we need everything to be in top shape—which is where you come in."

"Lauren." I hear the crack in my voice. "You don't need me. You need a professional. I'm not in top shape. I'm not even in middling shape—"

"You investigated robberies for one of the best insurance firms in the world. You're a professional. We're trying to get a prestigious jeweler to loan us pieces for Eva to wear at the pre-Oscar party and on the day of the awards. That's a lot of high-end loot to protect."

My throat tightens, even though I know Thorne & Company isn't likely to oblige. Ania told me they stopped loaning out pieces to Hollywood after her father became embroiled in several highly publicized legal fiascos where he sued big-name celebrities for not returning jewelry loaned to them for events. And after Cannes, where the Leopard stole the collection Ania had designed exclusively for stars to wear at the festival, there'd be even less reason for Thorne & Company to take the risk. They have a sketchy history with Tinseltown.

"Most reputable jewelers will assign someone to—" I start to say.

"We don't want just any ape on their payroll. Eva Elain is a star. She needs someone who understands discretion and can deal with overprivileged, demanding people like her. You handled clients for Lambert, who had their jewelry stolen. You know how they expect to be treated."

"I never dealt with movie stars when I worked for Lambert," I say, recalling Elizabeth Taylor's tirade directed at Ania in Cannes when Miss Taylor found out she had no jewelry to wear.

"Same as rich society ladies, except with more booze and sex," says Lauren dryly.

I have to laugh. "Really?"

"Really. Just think Julie Kimbell if she'd had a successful career as an actress."

"Ouch."

"You got that right. But before you think I'm offering you a lifetime of babysitting women who ought to know better, it's not permanent." She crushes out her cigarette and reaches into her pocketbook. "It's a limited contract. They'll announce the nominees in February, and the Oscars are on April 4th. We'll expect you by early March. The studio will cover all your expenses. That's plane fare, a car, and an apartment in Los Angeles, plus your salary." She pulls out a document. "Look it over."

I watch her set it on the table. She finishes her scotch and checks her watch. "Oh, boy. I have to go to my hotel and get some shut-eye. Long flight, and tomorrow I'm up to my ears in irate movie theater reps who aren't happy we're delaying the picture's European premiere. We don't like it any more than they do, but if we win an Oscar, then the box office is likely to double, so waiting to open abroad is the smart move."

She pauses. "Promise me you'll think about it, okay? You'd be doing us a huge favor. You can ring me at the Carlton with your answer. I'll be here for three days."

"Yes, I'll think about it." I accompany her to the door. "Want me to call you a cab?"

"No, I have a driver waiting for me in Earl's Court. I sent him to eat something while I came to see you. It's fine." She pulls on her coat and meets my stare. "You'll like Los Angeles. It's everything London isn't, and you really look like you need a change. What can go wrong?"

"You're asking me that after Venice? It was less than a month there."

"Oh." She winces. "Well, what are the chances of something like that happening again?"

I smile. "Probably none." As she turns to the door, I add, "And I owe you for Venice."

She ties her scarf around her head. "Friends don't call in debts." Then, rising on tiptoe, she kisses my cheek. "Don't be a stranger," she says as she always does when she says goodbye to me.

After she leaves, I pace to the window and watch her hurry down the street. A car pulls up, and she gets in, the vehicle turning to take her to her downtown hotel and business meetings.

She never mentions Ania. We never speak of it, though she knows I spent the first three months after Venice tracking down every lead I could until it became painfully clear that wherever she is, Ania doesn't want to be found. She has enough money to disappear, which is what she did. Lauren knows it, too, but she never brings it up.

This job offer is how she says it instead. She's not stupid, either. She's seen the direction I'm headed in and knows it won't turn out well. Dead-end jobs that cover my rent and too much whiskey at night. No life to speak of and no interest in one. Turning into a slob.

You'll like Los Angeles. It's everything London isn't, and you really look like you need a change. What can go wrong?

In my experience, things usually go wrong when I least expect it. As I pull out my bed from the sofa, I think she's right about one thing:

I need to make a change.

Chapter Two

Ania

As the plane takes off from Orly airport, I open my carryall and pull out the sketch pad and a box of colored pencils. I haven't taken a commission for over a year, and I feel rusty. And anxious. The fact is, I wouldn't have taken this one if I hadn't seen it as a possible pathway to helping me accomplish a goal that has eluded me for more than a year.

A very long and miserable year.

I pluck out the black pencil and stare down at the empty page. Since I first accepted this assignment, I've felt unequal to the task. How to create two suites of jewelry centered on a jungle theme without making them a poor imitation of Cartier?

Cartier's panther jewelry goes back to 1914, which I happen to know because I've been schooled in jewelry lore since I was a child. Other little girls read fairy tales at bedtime. My father told me how his friend, the gemologist George Kunz, had carried a gun to hunt amethysts in the Urals. He lulled me to sleep with the story of how Jean Baptiste Tavernier plucked the Hope Diamond out of an ancient stone sculpture with wild dogs nipping at his heels. Entertained me with tales of where the last tsar had hidden his still-lost cache of gold.

When it came to Cartier's menagerie, my father was snobbish, often reminding me that before the Duchess of Windsor put their diamond panther on her shoulder, only actresses and prostitutes wore figurative jewelry. And as far as he was concerned, it remained déclassée.

I always wondered if that was more his jealousy speaking and if he'd taken the moniker of *the Leopard* to remind people of his nemesis. Yes, Thorne & Company was one of the most prestigious, well-known jewelry houses in the world, but Cartier was unquestionably the greatest.

If I ever see him again, I will ask him—if I, in fact, figure out why he took on that particular sobriquet. For now, I need to concentrate on the job at hand.

I quickly sketch a leopard brooch and then study it. It looks like a bad copy of one created by Cartier. That won't do. I have to find a way to make this animal a signature Thorne piece. I crumple the paper and drop it into my carryall. I draw another and discard it, too, then begin another, which is no better.

My thoughts wander, making it hard to focus. It's not that I don't want to see my father again. I do. Desperately. In the year since we last saw each other, a brief, ominous encounter on a quay in Venice, I've never stopped searching for him. He wasn't in any of his old haunts, and none of his friends told me they had seen or talked to him—or at least they claimed they hadn't. Despite how devious my papa is, he still inspires great loyalty. Who among them was lying to me?

When my father left me that night on the Grand Canal as he jumped into a boat and drove away, he put me in a very precarious position with both the police and my lover. And I wanted to know why. He showed me why soon after. Now, more than twelve months later, I'm still enraged, but I can't help myself either. I'm worried about what might be coming. Where is he? Is he hiding out of choice or by necessity? He took a calculated risk by replacing the Lemon Twist with a glass replica and absconding from Venice with one of his most famous pieces, one intrinsically tied to him. The authorities have never recovered anything that the Leopard stole, but this was the first theft of something *he'd* created. Every time before, even my collection in Cannes, was someone else's work. To take the Lemon Twist might have placed him in a precarious position, too.

All these conflicting emotions wreak havoc on my sanity.

And it isn't just my father's disappearance that has me unsettled. I haven't seen Jerome since that ill-fated trip to Venice, either. I absconded from him.

I once had two men in my life. Now, both of them are missing. I'm hunting one and abandoned the other.

I sketch another leopard, this one even less interesting. I tear the sheet off the pad, toss it aside, and start again. What comes out next isn't an animal at all but a yellow glove with black spots. I shiver. The calling card of the greatest jewel thief in the last thirty years, at least according to the police. The glove the Leopard always left behind in the empty safe, jewel box, or on the floor of his victim's home.

To the world, he's a name without a face. But to me, he's Papa, and we have unfinished business.

The steward approaches. "Miss Thorne, we'll be serving lunch soon. What would you like to drink? I can offer you champagne. Wine? A soft drink?"

I accept the champagne. Maybe the alcohol will distract me from thinking about the men in my life—or those who used to be in it. I have work to do and very limited time to accomplish it. I spent four days in Paris discussing the unexpected commission from Segal Pictures with Jeanne Toussaint, Cartier's head designer since 1933.

Despite my father's disparagement of Cartier, he'd urged me to take an internship working for Madame Toussaint as one of several he set up for me before I went to work for him. She was an amazing mentor, one of the most talented women I've ever met, and a true original with contagious *joie de vivre*. She was the only person I could think of besides my father who could help me find my footing with this commission. Papa would never have accepted the commission on principle—he hated Hollywood—and that's why I did. I need to design a suite so spectacular that he can't possibly ignore it.

But that wasn't the only reason I flew to Paris. I wanted Madame Toussaint's blessing.

I've always prided myself on my originality. I've never copied another jeweler's style in my creations for Thorne, but I'd become afraid that it would appear as if I were mimicking Cartier no matter how I approached this new job. I needed to attract attention, not snide remarks that Ania Thorne was losing her edge. I wanted to honor Toussaint's work by creating something unmistakably mine. I had no idea how to do that. Failure wasn't an option—too much was riding on this.

I explained my dilemma over tea at the Ritz, steps from her office at Cartier's Rue de la Paix shop. Madame Toussaint told me her panthers had been copied so many times already, she took it as a compliment at this point. Somewhat relieved, I thanked her, though a copy wasn't my intent. She must have sensed it, for she said, "That's not all that's bothering you, is it, *ma cherie?*"

I could only say so much without disclosing what I knew about my father. I waved off her concern, saying what would make sense but not rouse suspicion: that I was having a hard time finding my inspiration. And that I kept seeing her panthers and not a way to design my own.

"Did I ever tell you how all this nonsense with the panthers began?" she asked.

I shook my head.

"It was a fluke. In 1913, Louis Cartier commissioned the artist George Barbier to create an advertising campaign to reflect a modern, worldly woman. I was acquainted with Barbier, and he asked me to model for him. At the time, the big cats were in vogue. Somehow, the wild animal had come to express the exuberant spirit of Paris after the war. A lover even gave me a panther coat." She laughed. "You know, I can't remember his last name now. But it was a fabulous fur, and I wore it everywhere. It's now said I was the first woman in Paris to wear a panther coat. Maybe, maybe not. Either way, I wore it to the studio to model for Barbier, and it gave him an idea. He called his illustration *Dame à la Panthère* and had me looking out at the viewer, seemingly unaware of a sleek black cat sitting at my feet. The drawing forged the first connection between Cartier and panthers."

Madame Toussaint pulled her purse into her lap, opened it, and withdrew an onyx cigarette case decorated with a diamond-and-onyx panther emerging from between two cypress trees.

"I'm sure I've shown this to you before, yes?" she asked.

I nodded. "But you never told me the story behind it."

"Monsieur Cartier had this made for me as a thank-you gift for modeling for that illustration." She pushed it toward me. "It was his first gift to me."

Madame Toussaint was known as *La Panthère* in jewelry circles. Gossip suggested that Monsieur Cartier had given her the nickname when they first became lovers. I watched how reverently she handled the case as she returned it to her pocketbook and felt a lump in my throat. At least she had something to remember her lover. I didn't even have one of Jerome's empty cigarette packs as a memento. But now was not the time for sentimentality. Jerome was gone, and I'd let him go. It was the only way to protect him.

I returned my attention to Madame. "What attracted you to panthers in the first place, before you were asked to pose or met Cartier?"

She sipped her tea, reflecting. "I've always spent much of my free time in museums. When I first came to Paris, I spent hours in the Louvre and fell in love with a painting by Corot called *Bacchante with a Panther*. I've gone back so many times to study that painting and always wonder why it speaks to me so strongly. Maybe we should go together. It might inspire you, as well."

We finished our tea, and as we walked to the museum, Madame told me about creating her first panther brooch for the Duchess of Windsor and how it spurred a trend.

"Since then, it's been said that Cartier is the panther, and the panther is Cartier. Now you have the wonderful challenge of making the animal yours. I have no doubt you will find your motivation, Ania."

Which is why I'm now thousands of feet in the air on a plane surrounded by discarded sheets of drawing paper, crumpled into angry little balls. How the hell am I supposed to put the Thorne stamp on the jungle beast and not just have my design look like a Cartier?

The steward arrives with my flute of champagne, and I put the pencil down and shift the sketch pad aside to make room for the plate with a *foie gras amuse bouche* on it. As I take a bite, I remember something Madame Toussaint said to me as we were in the museum, looking at her beloved painting.

"I'm drawn to art that expresses joy. I look at this painting and am certain Corot was delighted by the process of his creation. I recognize that in him because I feel it when I design." She looked at me, not voicing that it was how I used to feel, too, when I designed for her and then later on in the early years of working for my father.

That's my problem, I think as clouds fill the window and block out the sky. I've stopped finding joy in my work. But how can I anymore? My life has become a shadow of itself since Cannes, when the Leopard stole not only a collection I'd designed but robbed me of my illusions, as well. I discovered that my father was a master thief, a liar, and a deceiver. As difficult as that was to accept, it wasn't until Venice when he stole the Lemon Twist that I really understood the depth of what he was capable of. He took far more than the necklace. He set Jerome up to take the fall. He'd stolen my last shred of trust in him and destroyed it.

Where the hell is the joy in that? I wonder as the champagne sours in my mouth.

And then, all of a sudden, I see it. Madame Toussaint used joy as her muse, but that isn't an emotion currently available to me. Instead, I will use the emotion I have too much of: my desire for revenge. She'd focused on platinum and white diamonds to evoke sensuality. I'll use Thorne's signature yellow diamonds and gold to evoke cunning. My spotted cats will crouch in bushes and on tree limbs, waiting to spot their targets, ready to pounce. Her leopards' spots gave them a powerful uniqueness. Mine will aid them as they hide from their prey before they attack.

I'll design my leopard and become it. Hide in plain sight until I am ready to ambush my prey, and then I will pounce. The suite will indeed be spectacular, and it won't fail to attract attention, luring the one person I'm truly designing it for.

Yes, an actress will wear it, but it's bait for the real-life leopard I intend to take down.

Chapter Three

Jerome

Back in the good ole U S of A. I don't know the West Coast well, though. I was born and raised on the East Coast—and it's been almost twenty years since I set foot in the United States. I live in Europe now—if what I have been doing lately can be called *living*. After the war, coming home meant staying away. I had no family left. No wife or kids. Nothing waiting for me here. So, I moved to London because they speak English and…why not?

Los Angeles is immense, sprawling like spilled cake batter, and it looks like a cake, too: all pink and white with everything neon-frosted. Traffic is appalling. Glamour shots of movie stars in epic pictures seduce from billboards, advertising the blood of this city of dreams. It's certainly not London. Even in early March, the sun is so bright I have to wear sunglasses, and I'm sure my pasty complexion marks me as a foreigner from miles away.

LA's not a good-looking city, in my opinion. London can be dismal at times, but then Westminster Abbey or a dark-beamed pub that's been sitting on the same street for over four hundred years comes into view, and the city's ancient past colors the air. Los Angeles has no past. Carved out of the desert for make-believe, built on tinsel and celluloid, on the dreams of the thousands who flock here, hoping to one day see their name in lights, it's as much an illusion as the movies.

Lots of dreams and tons of disappointment. That's what colors the air here.

After the overseas flight, which I slept for most of, a studio car picks me up from the airport and takes me through the city to a wrought-iron gated lot with the name Segal Pictures etched into a faux-Roman archway that's as ostentatious as the pictures the studio produces.

Lauren gave me a publicity brief to review on the plane, listing a rundown of her father's studio's achievements. Founded in 1921, the studio survived the tumultuous transition from silent to talkies, but compared to its larger rivals MGM and Paramount, Segal Pictures doesn't have much to boast about, except for its tenacity. A few box-office hits, but none that reached the status of a classic, no *Gone with the Wind*. A few big-name stars, who wasted no time finishing out their contracts and moving to another studio for better pay and better roles. All in all, it looks like *The Treasure of Kilimanjaro* is their big-time ticket to the lasting acclaim that every studio strives for. If it can score an Oscar or two—Lauren's grapevine was right on the mark. The picture scored three nominations: Best Picture, Best Actress, and Best Director. If they win, Lionel Segal can retire a happy man, having seen his life's work rewarded by official industry recognition.

I haven't seen the picture yet myself, though I probably should now that I'm temporarily working for the studio.

Lauren comes out of the blocky white office building fronted by a manicured lawn like an incongruous park in the middle of an industrial complex. The grass is so green it looks fake to me, but then so does everything else here.

"Hey, you made it." She's in a trim beige skirt and jacket, looking crisp and efficient. She has her hair tied back with a scarf and her makeup subdued. The studio head's daughter at work. Guess when you're not in front of the camera or in a meeting, there's no point in getting dolled up. "How was the flight?"

"Not bad." I crack a smile, reaching into my jacket pocket. "Can I smoke?" Before leaving London, I made an effort to pick through my limited wardrobe and realized I needed to spend part of my advance salary retainer on some decent clothes. I splurged on a navy-blue suit, a tweed jacket, gray pleated trousers, several crisp, white shirts, and a few simple ties. But the tweed is starting to itch, and it's too heavy for LA's climate.

"Sorry, not here," Lauren says. "Pop hates it. You can smoke on the rest of the lot, though. Everyone does. But this is the business area, and

Pop laid down the law." She toes the grass. "He put in this lawn and benches for our employees, but no one ever uses them. Because you can't smoke here."

I chuckle. "I can wait."

"You have good timing." She motions toward the row of closed lots, where I see people hauling props on carts or grabbing a quick cup of coffee and a cigarette outside. "Eva is here. The jewelry is arriving later today for a fitting to see how it looks on her. She hasn't decided what she wants to wear for the party and the ceremony yet. She wants to see the jewelry first."

"Oh." I didn't expect to meet the star today. I'm rested enough from sleeping on the plane, if a bit heavy on the five-o'clock shadow, and I try to think of any pictures of hers that I've seen in case I need to make small talk. I come up blank. I haven't been much for going to the movies lately—or doing much of anything, to be honest.

Lauren gives me a smile. "Don't worry. Eva's a pain in the ass when it comes to her camera angles and her billing on the marquee, but she's okay otherwise. Like I said, think Julie Kimbell."

"Julie Kimbell was pretty much a total pain in the ass," I mutter as Lauren takes me into the office building. "She propositioned me on her ballroom floor."

"I know. I saw her doing it. Jeez, she hasn't changed a bit. Contessa or not, she still thinks she has to sleep her way to the top."

"All the talk of the casting couch," I ask, "is it really true?"

"Sure." Lauren shrugs. "Not here. I mean, Pop isn't a groper, and he doesn't like it in his studio. He says it's bad for business. But it's still Hollywood. Stars are like socialites, remember? Just with more booze and sex."

We enter a large room. It's almost empty save for a backdrop on the wall, lights on stands, a worktable, and a dressing table, along with a full-length mirror, and a rack hung with garment bags.

An auburn-haired woman in a white silk robe sits with her back to us at the dressing table, having her makeup applied. I hear her husky voice. "No. Too much rouge. I'm not a clown."

She catches sight of us in the mirror, and I see a surprisingly small face. I forget that in order to be blown up to ten times their usual size on the screen, actors tend to be small people. She's strikingly beautiful. Her green eyes have an exotic tilt to them. With her pale skin and short, tousled hair, she has something of a young, earthier Elizabeth Taylor look about her—which doesn't make me any less uncomfortable. Miss Taylor has a mean temper.

"Darling." She lifts a red-nailed hand to beckon Lauren. "Will you please tell this person—what's your name again?"

"Susan," intones the assistant in a long-suffering voice.

"Whatever. Tell her I'm not being photographed today so she can knock it off with the pancake foundation and rouge." Eva Elain shoots Susan-or-whatever a withering stare. As we approach, she bestows me with a thousand-watt smile that leaves me no doubt why she's a star. That kind of chemistry can't be manufactured. The dream factory can polish it to a high gloss, but the person has to be born with it first.

Eva Elain has a surplus to spare.

"Oh, my." Her drawl belies the glamour, a hint of Kentucky backwater not entirely erased by years of studio diction lessons. I like it, the glimpse of the redneck girl she used to be before becoming a name in lights. "Who's this tall drink of whiskey in tweed, of all things?"

"Jerome Curtis," says Lauren. "Jerome, this is Eva Elain. Eva, Jerome is the security professional we've hired to protect the jewelry. He'll be your bodyguard at the party and on the day of the awards."

Eva Elain flicks her hand at Susan and reaches for a cigarette, extending her silver monogrammed case to me. I take one, thinking I might as well—guess Pop Segal's no-smoking rules don't apply to his top star—and she lights it for me with a butane lighter. I'm surprised by it: a regulation army lighter, like the one I used to carry in my pocket during the war.

"So, tall, brooding, and handsome." She assesses me through a well-rehearsed *femme fatale* plume of smoke. "You protect the jewelry and screw the actress wearing it."

I sputter, coughing on my exhale. "Excuse me?"

Her smile widens. "Not literally. Or, not unless you want to."

Here we go.

Lauren snorts. "Eva, the come-hither is like rouge. Too much of it spoils the illusion."

"You can say that again." To my relief, Eva lets out a gusty laugh. "Can't say I don't earn my pay, though, can you?" She gives me a wink. "I was kidding. But it's good to know upfront which investment the studio chooses to protect. I might be the one nominated for an Oscar, but Papa

Segal hires a professional to make sure I don't run off with the Thorne loot."

Everything freezes for a moment. I feel the blood drain to my feet and then make an impossibly slow-motion turn to Lauren. "Thorne…?" I echo. I can't curb the accusatory edge in my voice.

Lauren says quietly, "I didn't know until the last minute. We asked Cartier and Tiffany's, as well as several other houses. I never expected Thorne to agree. They don't do this sort of thing."

"You might have told me," I say, feeling Eva's curious gaze moving between us.

"As I said, I didn't know until…Jerome, you'd already signed the contract with us. I figured you'd want to do it anyway, even once you knew."

"Did Ania design the pieces?" My voice catches on a snag. I can feel my heart pounding.

"I don't know. We only received word from the company that they could loan us two exclusive, original sets. I suppose we can ask when it gets here."

Ania must have designed them. There's no way Thorne & Company would agree to loan exclusive, original pieces for a nominated actress to wear in public and not have Ania involved. Despite my numerous attempts, I was never able to get through to Luke Westerly, aka Mr. Cologne, who's been running the company during Ania's leave of absence. It really pissed me off at the time that he refused to take my long-distance calls from London, though I also understood. Luke's loyalty is to Ania, first and foremost. If she told him not to communicate with me, he'd obey without question.

A secretary appears in the doorway. "Miss Segal, Mr. Westerly just arrived. Shall I show him up?"

My cigarette slips from my fingers to the floor. I stamp my foot down on it.

Lauren nods. "Yes, please." Then she meets my incredulous stare.

Eva grinds out her cigarette in an ashtray on the dressing table and turns resolutely to the mirror. "More rouge," she orders Susan. "It's starting to look like the occasion might require it."

When Luke walks into the room, I can see he's as stunned as I am. Not that it's easy to see. The man is picture-perfect in a light seersucker suit, ideal for LA, a flagrant pink handkerchief peeping from his jacket's upper pocket. His wave of chestnut-colored hair is silvering at his temples as if he specially designed it that way, and his broad-shouldered, gym-toned body is without a hint of a paunch, even though he's middle-aged. He's the kind of debonair New Yorker that frequents only the best restaurants, wears a vintage Thorne wristwatch, and would never be caught dead in public in blue jeans. He's always made me feel like a slob. Like Ania, the guy is way out of my league.

He pauses for a second that says everything, his hazel eyes widening as he takes me in.

Then he ignores me to set the case he's carrying onto the worktable. My stomach plummets as I recognize it, identical to those he brought to Paris during our aborted attempt to catch the Leopard. He gives Eva a gleaming smile that has her eyeing him up and down as if he's her next co-star. The seductive extension of her hand, which he actually kisses as though we're in some royal production, has me biting back a smile. She's wasting her come-hither on him. Luke Westerly doesn't play for her team.

"Miss Elain, this is a pleasure. I'm such a fan," he says in his posh, upper-crust eastside accent. The man's a charmer, if you like that sort of swank. "I've seen all your pictures."

"Oh, I hope not *all* of them." She gives him her thousand-volt smile that looks especially lit for the camera. "Some of them really shouldn't be seen."

Luke returns the smile. He doesn't lack for wattage, either, and I'm about to bark a barrage of questions at him when he motions to the case.

"Shall we? I think you're going to look divine in these."

Eva leaps to her satin-slippered feet with the greed of the backwater girl she still is at heart. It's actually funny to see her Hollywood luster crumble like paste as she nearly rubs her hands together in glee. No fool, our Miss Elain. Original Thorne pieces will make her stand out among her fellow nominees like the reigning queen she is at the box office.

Lauren makes an impatient gesture at me to join them, though I feel rooted in place. I lurch to the table, catching a whiff of Luke's expensive scent—I dubbed him Mr. Cologne for a reason—and he turns the combination locks on the case, clicking it open.

Eva lets out a delighted gasp.

The pieces are Ania's. The moment I see them, there's no doubt in my mind. Only she could have designed them.

Jewelry that suggests the jungle, with a teasing hint of stealth. I have to focus. My pulse is throbbing, and what I first see are blades of grass, fashioned from filigree emerald sprays on a choker necklace, which Luke removes to clasp around Eva's throat as she holds up her hair. Halfway across her neck, the emerald grass sprays part to reveal the head of a leopard peeking out—gold diamonds on a gold head with black enamel spots.

The beast hides there, waiting for you to see him.

The ring is a large, ten-carat emerald that Luke slips onto Eva's finger. No hint of the leopard at first until she holds it up to the light and I see that the sides of the ring are set with gold pavé diamonds and onyx spots. Again, the animal hiding. Waiting. Tempting.

Eva glides to the full-length mirror, pulling down her robe to bare her shoulders and admire the necklace against her skin.

"The dress has to be low-cut in gold or black," she tells no one in particular as if there were any doubt she'd want to show off her world-famous cleavage. Susan-or-whatever moves to the rack of garments, searching through them as Lauren says, "The Balenciaga, maybe. Or the Dior."

I take the moment of distraction to stare at Luke as the assistant locates the dresses. He gives me an apologetic look that I'm not buying for a second.

"I need to talk to you," I hiss.

"I'm quite certain you do," he replies. "But not here. Not now."

"Listen—" I have to curb my tone. Eva coos as the Dior or Balenciaga is removed from its bag. She drops her robe without hesitation, revealing nude-colored lingerie and a garter belt.

Luke sets a hand on my sleeve that surges my temper. As I start to wrench away, he forces me to turn around with him so we have our backs to the star as Lauren and Susan help her into the dress. "Later," he says.

"Later? Like when? Look, I know something's up. Ania—" My voice breaks suddenly. "She's up to something. The jewelry—"

"What do you think?" Eva calls out with a slight petulance that has Luke turning around to her with an expansive smile.

She's in a very low-cut gown, the bustier embroidered in some kind of beading, and the wide skirt billowing from her hips to her calves.

"The Dior is perfect," Luke pronounces.

"Really?" Eva frowns. "Shouldn't I try on the Balenciaga just to be sure?"

"Of course," Luke says. He's nothing if not a gentleman who can appreciate indecisiveness.

"And is this all of it?" Eva snaps her fingers at Susan to unzip the back of the Dior dress.

"No. This is the suite for the party. We have another designed for the awards. It's not ready yet but should be here by tomorrow. Same theme," adds Luke.

"Oh," says Eva. She gives me another wink. "You'll have your work cut out for you, handsome. When the other gals get a look at these shiners, they'll want to tear them off me."

She's in her lingerie again, so we turn around to give her some privacy.

"Leopards?" I mutter at Luke. "Interesting choice."

He nods. "It's appropriate. The nominated picture is an African adventure, after all."

"Like hell this is about the picture."

He slides his gaze to me. "I realize you're very upset with Ania, but don't expect me—"

"You don't understand shit." The fury in my tone finally gets through to him. "We need to talk in private. There are some things you should know. About Ania. About the Leopard."

Again, it's not easy to see, but I can tell he's taken aback. "What do you suggest?"

"Dinner tonight. Just the two of us."

"Oh?" He arches an eyebrow, and I glare at him.

"Don't get any ideas, buddy."

"I wouldn't dream of it," he replies. "But I suppose I do owe you dinner, at least."

"And an explanation, seeing as you never bothered to take my calls. Meet me at 456 Wiltshire. The studio put me up in an apartment there. Six-thirty. There's a burger joint down the street."

"Burgers at six-thirty? Really?" Luke turns to Eva, who's preening in a gold, off-the-shoulder sheath gown with an asymmetrical cape. "The Balenciaga is lovely, Miss Elain, but I think it's a bit busy. Perhaps the simplicity of the Dior is preferable?"

"Yes." Eva sounds disappointed. She's a star. The busier the outfit, the better. "I guess so."

She nods to Susan, and I fix my eyes on Luke. "Really. Don't think of not showing up."

"Oh, Mr. Curtis." He sighs. "You always were a bit too suspicious for your own good. If I say I owe you dinner, then I owe you dinner. But not burgers. I don't eat them. I'll pick you up at seven-thirty. Please try to wear something less…rustic. Not that Scotsman's kilt on your back. I'm taking you to the Brown Derby for dinner, and they have a strict dress code, which, in your case, means a decent coat and tie. Now, if you'll excuse me." He walks away to attend to Eva and speak with Lauren.

I feel my hands bunch into fists and have to consciously relax.

Leopard jewelry. *Ania,* what *are you doing now?*

Chapter Four

Ania

As I drive up the hill, I almost forget and go straight to our house instead of taking a left to the caretaker's cottage. Pulling into the garage, I hoist the bag of groceries and start up the steps. The sack is heavy, and not knowing the bumps and uneven surfaces of the stones leading down to the door, I trip and fall, the bag coming with me.

Damn. The sound of breaking glass and the instant scent of oranges—as in, juice, as in breakfast—seeps out.

I'm not myself. Since my arrival in Los Angeles, this whole effort has been—well, more like an ordeal in a city that's never been one of my favorites. The stress of my double-mission is taking its toll. As if designing two suites of jewelry in record time isn't enough, I'm also hiding out, planning for a denouement, and not sure if I can pull it off or how I'll feel in the aftermath.

I need a glass of wine. Or two. That will help calm my nerves, ease the pain in my knee from my fall, and get me through another night. I only have four more nights to endure, and half the jewelry is still on the bench, being finished. Just thinking of how behind I am on the job increases my stress level, though it's a reflexive habit. I'll deliver the second suite on time, and my company will get the publicity for it, even if I might be—

No. Best not to think about that.

I gather up the spilled groceries—except for the juice, which I'll deal with later—and make my way inside. First things first. I pull the bottle of wine from last night out of the cabinet and pour a glass. I'm surprised to see it only amounts to a few sips. That's when I realize I forgot to stop at the liquor store. It isn't like me to forget. Miss Organization has become quite disorganized. And, apparently, she's drinking too much. I'm not usually someone given to excess when it comes to alcohol.

Now, I'll have to go up to the house to fetch another bottle. I look out the window. I still have at least fifteen minutes before sunset, enough time to get up there and back without turning on any lights. I'm not thrilled about taking the wine; I can't let anyone notice my presence here. Although even if my father does show up unexpectedly, he isn't the sort to count bottles of wine to see if any were pilfered. Besides, if anyone deserves to have his precious wine stolen, it's him. His wine and more. Much more.

Stopping myself from spiraling into ruminations, I put the milk, lettuce, eggs, and bacon in the refrigerator and then make my way up to the main house to avail myself of a bottle of something red and robust.

No artist is only an artist in his or her field. A painter friend does impressionistic landscapes and sets his dinner table with a unique sensitivity to light and color. A playwright I know dresses with a decidedly dramatic flair. My father's residences are all reflections of his art, but nowhere is his sense of design more on display than Thorne House in the Hollywood Hills.

He built and completed it after my mother passed. Simpler than our residence in New York and a reflection of the mid-century modern architecture so popular among the avant-garde, the house is situated on a nearly vertical precipice—a seemingly impossible feat that Papa and the architect were inspired to defy. The floor-to-ceiling glass walls and steel foundation create the illusion of a structure cantilevered over the hills as if suspended on air. Out by the pool, it feels as if you could step off the deck and drop a thousand feet. But it's all an optical illusion; the ledge extends over a drop of only one foot to the rock shelf. The house itself is all right angles with no soft curves.

And as befits a jeweler, the home reflects light like a jewel. From its shape against the skyline to how the sun comes through the glass walls, the light inside is ever-changing, painting the walls at different times of day in various hues. Everything about the domicile is true to my father's aesthetic and his claims about this city: that LA is an illusion, and everyone who lives here has an angle. And yet, he always said that of all the places he's lived, none pleased him more. I think it's because it holds no memories of the past, of my mother. It's all his, just endless views of a sprawling city he detested and set himself to conquer. One that proved to be his downfall in the end.

"We are all in the gutter, but some of us are looking at the stars."

My father's favorite quote is spelled out. And nowhere are Oscar Wilde's words truer than in this house.

Inside, I head for the wine cabinet and find a Chateau Laffite that will do the trick. Yes, it's expensive, but the rack doesn't have anything *less* expensive. While I'm rooting about, I check the back of the cabinet for anything unusual.

The light is fading. I need to return in daylight.

Grabbing my bottle, I stop to stare out at the astonishing sunset. Vivid reds, oranges, and ambers streak across a cerulean blue sky. I'll never design a piece of jewelry that can compare to nature's palette.

"As long as you don't stop trying," I hear my father say, his words of encouragement whenever I felt defeated by my efforts.

Well, Dad, you'll be happy to know I'm not giving up in my efforts to right this wrong.

I don't say it aloud. He's not here. But he is. He's everywhere in this house.

After a few more moments of admiring the sky, I remind myself not to linger. As much as I wish I could stay and drink my wine by the pool while watching the fiery sun sink behind the hills, I can't. The steps down to the cottage are treacherous in the dark, and I've already fallen once today. The compound has three separate structures. There's this three-thousand-square-foot, three-bedroom house with its astonishing pool hanging over the hills. Then the pool house, a small building below us for changing, taking showers, and where the guts of the pool reside behind a door. Finally, one hundred feet past the garden is the caretakers' cottage. A compact, two-bedroom bungalow without any views. But it has an attached garage, which is convenient for the live-in couple.

Benjamin and Debra Miller are now on holiday, visiting their daughter in North Dakota. They believe that my father gave them the unexpected trip because they received a letter from him with two paid plane tickets and a note that they deserved a vacation. They'll probably discover that the tickets came from me at some point in the future. But by then, it won't matter.

Meanwhile, I've moved into the cottage. I'm driving their station wagon and sleeping in their bedroom, with sheets I brought down from the main house because why sleep on low-count cotton when high-count Egyptian is just a short walk away?

I've spent the last three weeks keeping pretty much to the same schedule as I have today.

I rise, brew coffee, head up to the main house, and swim for forty-five minutes. Then I shower in the pool house, return to the cottage, dress, and drive into town to work with the jewelers on the pieces for Segal Pictures. Then it's back to the house, usually around three in the afternoon, when I settle down for the other work that I'm doing here in LA.

I'm on a treasure hunt.

Looking at the fairly simple house with glass walls, no one would think it had many hiding places, but my father never lacked imagination. So, I know that a cabinet might have a secret panel built into it. Or that a bathroom tile can be lifted. My father boasted that he envisioned this house all by himself, a refuge for him when he was in LA, and he only employed the architect to bring the vision to life. He took pride in its construction. If he concealed the evidence of his crimes anyplace in the world, it's most likely here, where no one would think to look for it.

Thus far, I've lifted every rug, emptied every cabinet, and knocked on every wall, trying to find his secret lair. I thought I had found it three times.

In the master bedroom, after shoving the bed nearly two feet to the left, I found a low cabinet built into the wall that's invisible with the bed in its proper position. As soon as I saw it, I assumed I'd hit pay dirt, but the cabinet was shallow and empty. In a corner of the living room, there's a bar with four stools. When I wiggled off the stools' padded seats, I discovered that the metal bases were hollow—perfect hiding places. But they, too, were empty.

Then, in the library where my father often did his design work, I discovered a trapdoor to a small recess under the rug beneath his desk. Several jewelry boxes were inside it. I held my breath as I opened each one. The first contained a basic Thorne curb-chain bracelet in steel—a sample worth nothing save for its historical value. In the next was a turquoise cocktail ring missing most of its stones, equally worthless. The last box had a pair of thin, broken gold hoops, also of no value. I'm still not sure why he kept any of it. I also couldn't ascertain what the recess had been made for, other than as a place to store samples he used as references. But finding the baubles he'd left here, neglected, spiraled my apprehension.

Ever since the hunt started in Cannes, I've realized that I don't know him at all.

Leopards are the least social of the big cats; they keep to themselves, living in the brush around rock outcroppings. They either ambush their prey or stalk it, always getting as close as possible before pouncing. They don't chase their quarry but rather use surprise to catch and drag their kill up into a tree, where they hide it from scavengers.

If the house has three hidden places, there may be more. There has to be someplace here where my father hid his loot over the years.

Where is the Leopard's tree?

Chapter Five

Jerome

The Brown Derby sounds like the kind of pretentious, look-at-me-I'm-a-star place that Los Angeles revels in. With a dress code to boot, at least, according to Luke. I'm not looking forward to it as I pick through my wardrobe for my least British-looking jacket and a narrow black tie. At the last minute, after surveying myself in my studio-rented apartment's utilitarian mirror—pasted to the inside of the closet door—I decide on a black shirt instead of a white one to match my tie and pleated slacks. The coat is light gray wool, so I assume I look like an undertaker until Luke picks me up in an ostentatious, very oversized white Cadillac convertible, of all things, and gives me an approving smile that shows off his perfect teeth. The guy never smokes, either, like Ania, so they have these inhumanly unstained teeth.

"You heeded my advice," he remarks, gunning the car to gut-heaving speed toward North Vine, expertly navigating the glut of evening traffic as if he'd been born here.

"You should slow down," I tell him. "It's not New York."

"It most certainly is not." He glances at my hand, clutching the edge of the seat. "If it were, we'd be taking a car service. I never drive anywhere in New York."

"Well, after Paris, you should still slow down," I reply tersely. He was in a car crash in Paris that put him in the hospital. You would think he'd remember it.

"That was Paris. When in LA…"

The Brown Derby is located in Hollywood, of course. He zooms up and halts at the curb of a Spanish, mission-style building, leaving the car for the valet to park while he escorts me into the restaurant.

"Mr. Westerly, your table is ready," oozes the maître d'. Thorne & Company clout gets you the best seating anywhere you go.

It's not just a table, though there are plenty of those cluttering the tiled floor. We have a prestigious brown leather booth with framed cartoons mounted overhead, depicting famous people who I assume eat here. Cigarette smoke hangs thickly in the air. The place is packed, but to my eyes, it looks like an upper-class burger joint with an overpriced menu. When I look over the options, I almost laugh. And so it is: they serve burgers, too, though they call them *hamburger sandwiches.*

"The Cobb salad is delicious," Luke says. "And famous. Supposedly, it was invented here."

"A cheeseburger," I tell the waiter. "Medium-rare. With fries. Not too salty, please."

Luke smiles as he orders the delicious, supposedly-invented-here salad. "Suspicious and stubborn, too."

"I've had it up to my eyeballs with all the famous crap," I say irritably, thinking I sound just like the slob I think I am whenever I'm around him. "Everything here is famous. Or wants to be."

"Welcome to LA." He lifts his wine glass. He ordered a bottle of a crisp white vintage when I could have really used a scotch on the rocks. "I was wondering why you were here. Working for Segal Pictures as their hired security. Doesn't quite seem your style, does it?"

"No?" I passed on the wine, waving over the waiter to order my scotch. I'm not going to sip prissy white wine with a greasy burger. "What? You think I should be guarding jewelry warehouses in London like a German shepherd?"

"How quaint." Luke reclines in the booth, lacing his fingers and displaying a pair of very pricey vintage Thorne opal cufflinks. Cufflinks. That's the kind of guy he is: one who wears opal cufflinks to an upper-class burger joint. "I was referring to your significant expertise. I should think that guarding spoiled movie stars like a German shepherd isn't your preferred line of work."

"Not that it's any of your business, but the salary is definitely my preferred line of work. Ania left me high and dry in Venice. I quit my job at Lambert to be with her."

"Ah." He winces. "Right to the tumultuous heart of it."

The server delivers our food soon after.

"Can you also quit the upper eastside attitude for tonight?" I say, digging in. I'm famished. I didn't eat lunch, trapped all afternoon with Eva Elain and her indecision over which dress to wear. Lauren invited me out afterwards; guess she felt bad about it, too. When I told her that I was having dinner with Luke, she gave me a curious look that made me want to inform her that I don't swing for his team, though she damn well knows it and was just yanking my chain.

"Fine, no posh words for tonight." Luke eats with gusto. Dress code and vintage cufflinks aside, he has a robust appetite. I suddenly recall Ania picking like a bird at two pieces of arugula under a tablespoon of goose pâté or deboned fish that she called a meal.

My heart clenches. "Have you seen her?"

Luke dabs his mouth with the cloth napkin. "Not since you and she went to Venice."

"Not even once?" I ask.

"If I tell you I haven't seen her, you're going to have to believe me, Mr. Curtis."

"Jerome. I think we're past the formalities by now."

"Indeed." He pours himself more wine and orders me another scotch, though I haven't finished the one I have. I'm determined not to drink too much. I need to keep my mind clear.

"I haven't seen her at all," he goes on. "We've spoken over the telephone, but she's apparently elected to go into hiding like her father. Not her style, either," he adds. "To up and leave oversight of the company to me. I appreciate her trust in me, I honestly do, but it's been over a year now. And while I can't complain about the salary, the workload is overwhelming. The board is also starting to ask about whether she intends to return. I've assured them that she does."

I stare at him. "She didn't design those pieces for the studio, then?"

"You saw them yourself. It precipitated your demand for our get-together, yes? She did the designs personally. She even went to Paris to consult with a friend who worked with Cartier. She pounced at the opportunity after it arrived, though I mentioned it to her in passing. I never thought she'd agree. Again, it's not her style. Nor was it her father's. Virgil detested playing jeweler to the stars and ingrained the same aversion in his daughter. But after that unfortunate incident in Cannes…" Luke exhales. "I suppose she felt it necessary to earn back some goodwill. Hollywood may be tawdry and excessive, but our Los Angeles branch does very good business. We can't afford to ignore our marquee clientele, much as we'd prefer to."

She designed the pieces. I knew she had, but the confirmation doesn't reassure me.

"How did she do it?"

"Design the pieces?" He glances at me in surprise over a forkful of salad.

"Yeah. I mean, if she's not going into the office and is hiding away…"

"She sent over her sketches. It's not uncommon. I oversaw the purchase of the materials she required while she parceled the gemstones. Then I organized our workroom here for her to use—" He pauses at my startled expression. "You didn't know she was in LA?"

"No. Is she?" My voice is very low, almost emotionless. I'm surprised by it.

"I thought you already knew." He sounds concerned now. "I thought that was the actual reason you took the job for the studio. I won't interfere, Jerome. Like you said, it's none of my business. I think Ania made a mistake, treating you as she did, but I can't take sides in her personal affairs."

"You think she made a mistake?" All of a sudden, my burger tastes rancid. "Really?"

"I do." He fixes me with his gaze. "Contrary to what you think, I believe you were very good for her. I've never seen her so…involved before, not in something other than her work."

"Not even with Mr. Lockjaw Aviation Heir?"

"Hugh Lockling?" Luke chuckles. "He might be ideal for a first romance—all that inherited money and quite the physique to go with it—but he could never handle Ania as his wife. To be frank, I didn't think any man could until you came along."

"And she dumped me."

"Well." He resumes eating his salad, looking somewhat uncomfortable. "She didn't consult me on her decision. And I can't take sides."

"You might have to," I say, bringing him to a halt.

"Absolutely, not." He pushes his salad aside with an air of finality. "I'm very sorry that she broke up with you. I wish she hadn't, and when she told me she had, I wasn't consoling. Because I like you, Jerome Curtis. Though I shouldn't. You're precisely what she needs. She grew up under the immense shadow of a domineering father, so she had to learn very early on not to let herself be pushed around. She'll not tolerate another Virgil Thorne in her life, and who can blame her? You're not anything like him, except perhaps in your suspicious obstinacy, so I thought you could give her the happiness she doesn't think she needs. But that is as far as it goes. I will *not* be put in the middle of her love affair gone sour. She's very dear to me. I've known her since she was a girl and I consider us to be best friends. But she's also my boss."

"Well, your best friend and boss is in deep shit," I say. "From her father's immense shadow."

"I doubt that." Luke starts to lift his hand to beckon the waiter. "Virgil is retired now. He hates it, I'm sure, but he has nothing to do with the company. Ania runs it and—"

"He's the Leopard."

Luke falters when the waiter hustles over. "Two chocolate mousses, please. And coffee for both of us." He cuts off my protest that I still have the rest of my scotch to finish. "You will have dessert and coffee and explain your outrageous defamation."

I hadn't intended to state it so bluntly. It just came out. He gets under my skin, and while I know I should relax because we're not in any competition, I realize that, to me, we sort of are. He's known Ania since she was a child and worked under Virgil Thorne before transferring under her. She entrusted him with her company and clearly trusted him with word of our breakup. The guy likes matadors in tight pants, but she relies on him utterly, and I resent him for it.

"It's not defamation." I lower my voice, though the restaurant is full of clanking silverware and conversations. No one could overhear us if they tried. "He's the thief that stole her jewelry in Cannes and ran you off the road in Paris. He then came after us in Venice and tried to set me up to take the fall for the Lemon Twist. He almost succeeded."

Luke stirs cream into his coffee and spoons up some chocolate mousse. "I don't believe it."

Of course, he doesn't. So, I tell him everything I know. And I see as I do that the mousse starts to taste as rancid as the last few bites of my burger did for me.

He goes silent, swallowing. "She…she *confronted* him at their penthouse in New York?"

"I arrived after he'd left, but, yeah, she did. She went after him. She's not stopped going after him since. Venice was her plan, not mine. Steal that particular necklace to get his attention. She got his attention, all right. But he turned the tables on her. Lured us to a glass factory in Murano and left us a fake Lemon Twist. Ania made sure that I knew it. The necklace was the only thing she left behind in the palazzo. I threw it against a wall. It shattered into pieces. A perfect replica."

"My God." He looks green around his well-moisturized cheeks. "It's…incredible. Unbelievable. Why would he do something so insane? It makes no sense."

"Look." I take out my cigarettes. Screw it. Everyone else is smoking in the restaurant except Luke. "I don't have time to analyze his motivations. You know him much better than I do, so *you* figure it out. Later. She designed those leopard pieces for the studio. Now, that's a come-find-me invitation if I've ever seen one. Ania is still after him. She won't stop until he's in jail or one of them is dead. Do you understand? Because I'm not kidding around."

He nods slowly as though he's having difficulty absorbing it. I feel a pang of sympathy for the guy. It's a lot to hear from someone who is, more or less, his boss's ex-boyfriend. "And you think she's doing it again?"

"That would be my bet. We need to find her. Fast."

"And do what? If what you say is true, she's not about to throw up her hands and surrender. Ania is even more stubborn than you are when she puts her mind to something."

"Don't I know it." I flick ash onto my coffee saucer, seeing as there is no ashtray on the table. "But you set up that workroom for her, right? So where is it?"

"She's not there anymore. She finalized the pieces days ago. The awards-night suite got delayed, but it's being prepped for delivery now—polished and packed up. I went to the workroom myself yesterday to check on it when I arrived from New York. No one's seen her."

"Damn," I curse. "But she was here. Maybe she still is. Where would she go, Luke? Think."

He does. He eats most of his mousse, drinks his coffee, and doesn't say a word until I think he won't. I was expecting too much from him. Her acting president while she is away, his ultimate loyalty is to her and her company. Not to mention, he is doubtlessly stunned by the blows I've just delivered and not about to take me by the hand and lead me to Ania.

Then he says, "She never told me where she was staying. As I said, she's been acting like her father. Keeping secrets. I'm used to it from both of them. It's how they are. But…"

"But?" I lean to him.

"Virgil keeps a private residence here. A house overlooking the canyon. He had it custom-built after Ania's mother died. It was supposed to be their getaway from East Coast winters. A place for them to heal. It didn't turn out that way. Virgil created too much chaos with his lawsuits against the stars and the studios, and Ania is a New Yorker to her marrow. He used the house far more often than she ever has."

"She'd still stay there, though," I say. "While she's in LA. Why wouldn't she?"

"She wouldn't for all sorts of reasons. She booked a hotel the last few times she traveled here on business. The house is up in the hills, and she hates driving. Ania always prefers taking a car service like most civilized people." He beckons the waiter again, this time for the check. "But it's the only place I can think of in a pinch."

He gives me a pensive look. "I'll take you there. But let me be clear: I'm doing this for Ania. I won't see her put herself in danger. Virgil should pay for what he's done, but not on her back. He's taken quite enough from her already as far as I'm concerned." His voice hardens. "I'd like to confront him myself. I'd show him how to behave."

"I really appreciate it," I say as we stand to leave.

"Don't thank me yet. It's unlikely she's at the house. She must despise him, and that house is a monument to his ego. She never liked it there and probably dislikes it more now. But as I said, you're in a pinch."

"*We* are in a pinch. It's still the company you work for."

"Must you remind me?" Luke sighs again. "Let's just go there and hopefully put an end to this insanity before it gets entirely out of hand."

Chapter Six

Ania

I knew there wouldn't be a decent hotel room in all of Los Angeles with the Oscar ceremony taking place in three days, so I didn't even try to look for something out of the way. At this time of the night, I had no choice but to drive directly to the Pink Palace—my childhood name for the famed Beverly Hills Hotel—and lie about who I was. It was the only way I figured I could get a room at this late date, and I needed one fast. To regroup. To think. To try and figure out what I had seen and what it meant.

"The light switches are here, Miss Mabeson," says the bellman, who brought me to the room.

"Thank you," I say. I just want him to leave so I can sink into the couch and ruminate.

"And if you want room service, it's available all night."

I nod. I suddenly realize I haven't eaten since my early lunch. I missed dinner and then—

"Is there anything else?"

He's waiting for his tip. I hand him a bill. Enough but not too much. I don't want to stand out.

After I lock the door behind him, I turn to inspect the pink-and-green living room. Inviting, if a bit on the gaudy side as far as colors go.

But glamorous while still being comfortable. Lots of tufted pillows on the couch and heavy drapes for privacy. Lush plants for a touch of hominess.

I drop onto the couch and pull one of the pillows to my chest. I want to cry. Or scream. Not sure which, I do neither, focusing instead on tomorrow since I'm not quite ready to think about tonight.

In retrospect, it's convenient that I'm staying here since this is precisely where they're holding tomorrow night's pre-Oscar party. But it's also dangerous. Too dangerous? The scene of the planned crime would never have been my first choice for accommodations. Hardly the place to hide out if you don't want to get caught. Yet here I am. Staying in a bungalow that had become available because some out-of-town star had an unfortunate appendicitis attack and had to cancel his trip to hopefully collect his little gold statuette.

Instead, *I* have his room, one of the largest cottages on the property, hidden in the deep recesses of the hotel's jungle-like grounds. The bungalow has a separate entrance, which is perfect should anything go wrong tomorrow. A stroke of luck—something I've been running short of lately.

I check my watch, surprised that it's already ten-thirty. Tomorrow will be an insanely busy and stressful day. I need to get some rest. But I'm not tired. I call room service to order a pot of chamomile tea and some toast. I had dinner ready at the house—my tuna sandwich is still on the kitchenette counter in the caretakers' cottage, probably being devoured by flies by now. But eating was the last thing on my mind when I raced out after seeing Luke and Jerome pull up to the house.

With a rush of pure adrenaline, I threw everything into my suitcase and bolted out the back way. Somewhere in the back of my mind, I must have suspected that I might need to escape fast because I'd started parking the Millers' station wagon on the street. But I always imagined if there were an intrusion, it would be my father. It wasn't. And now I hope that if they heard me leave, they assumed it was just an arbitrary vehicle on the road instead of me making a getaway.

Jeez. So many words I'd never used in life before Cannes are now part of my daily vocabulary. *Steal. Bait. Heist. Getaway. Hideout. Setup.*

While I wait for the tea, I unpack to make sure I took what I will need for tomorrow's event. I'm surprised I had the presence of mind to add my toiletries, along with my disguise. All I'd been thinking about was getting out of there. The sooner I got away from those two men, the sooner I could breathe. And I had to breathe. It's how we stay alive. Even if there's not much I care about staying alive for these days, except for having my final showdown with my father once and for all.

The knock on the door startles me. Then I remember my room service order. I leave the open suitcase to let in the waiter. He's carrying a silver tray in that precise manner required by the best hotels, and I find myself observing him, taking mental notes on how he sets the tray on the coffee table and hands me the check, efficient and courteous without direct eye contact.

I need to do the same thing tomorrow night.

I give him a tip. Like with the bellman, not too little or too much—neither a cheapskate nor extravagant enough to cause any muttering among the hotel staff. I don't want to draw any attention if things go wrong, and the police make inquiries. At best, those who attended me will remember a bedraggled woman named Margaret Mabeson, who arrived and left unexpectedly.

A client and good friend of mine, Selma Mabeson, is a frequent guest at this hotel, so using her name in hindsight probably wasn't the smartest thing to do. But upon arrival, I went blank and heard myself telling the front desk that I was Mrs. Mabeson's niece and assistant and needed a room for a few days. She's so well-known here they didn't require payment in advance since she books on credit.

Such is the value of having friends at the top of the heap in society. Though if the police *do* happen to ask, Selma Mabeson will be very displeased to hear that someone dared to impersonate a niece she doesn't have. I should have come up with a less conspicuous alias, but no other would have gotten me this room or, indeed, any other in the hotel.

Door shut, waiter gone, I pour the tea and spoon in some sugar. I've heard it's good for shock. And I am still very much in shock. Finally, I let myself settle down to ruminate.

What the hell just happened? Had Luke and Jerome really been getting out of a car together in front of my father's house? What were they doing there at night?

I know why Luke is in Los Angeles. He's delivering the jewelry and ensuring Thorne & Company is well represented. But why go to my father's house—with Jerome, of all people? And why is Jerome even in LA? Last I heard, at least according to the private eye I hired to keep tabs on him, he was working in London. Not good jobs, and nothing like what he used to do or deserves, but at least I knew he was safe. Because, of course, I've been checking on him. I'm worried. It was my fault that he quit his job at Lambert Securities. My fault that he almost ended up in an Italian prison for the theft of the Lemon Twist. My fault that he has—or had—feelings for me.

Except it isn't all my fault. He knew the risks. But still, it is my fault for falling for him, encouraging him, and thinking I could have some kind of actual long-term relationship with a semi-sweet happy finale.

All I managed to do was drag him into my family chaos and criminal activities. I made such a disaster of it that I had no choice but to abandon him in Venice. I consoled myself with the reminder that he's a big boy, a war veteran. If anyone could fend for themselves in a foreign country, it was him. But I knew he'd be devastated, and I worried about him anyway. He's no doubt smoking too much and probably drinking heavily, too. And judging by how often he called my office—according to the messages my secretary took—and the numerous other calls he made to Luke—none of which Luke answered—I knew he was very angry with me.

Luke, too. He hadn't been pleased when I told him about the breakup. I can still remember his exasperated sigh. *"Ania, darling, why? I hate to say this, but a man like him doesn't come along every day. Or every year, for that matter. He's one of a kind. I thought you were so happy with him, off on your extended whirlwind romantic vacation."*

He heard me out, of course: my rehearsed if faltering excuse that Jerome and I were too different to survive the long-haul and that it was better to call it quits before one of us started resenting the other. I told Luke that my wealth was off-putting to Jerome, and he really wasn't the man for me, one of a kind as he may be. Hamburger and filet mignon don't belong on the same menu.

"Hugh Lockling was filet mignon," Luke then replied, catching me off guard. *"A prime cut of beef with his own fortune to spare. And I agreed completely when you pulled the plug on your engagement to him. Ania, this isn't about money. Jerome never struck me as one who cared about that. It's about you. You refuse to let a man get too close. As soon as they do, you push them away and run out the door. Without leaving a forwarding address, I might add."*

Ironic to recall his words now, seeing as how I just did that very thing. And I didn't answer his uncharacteristic rebuke on the phone that day, either. He didn't say anything more about it. We simply went on to discuss business. He mentioned our quarterly report—profits were up— and the offer from Segal Pictures, which I told him I would consider. He must have been surprised, as he should have been. My father's lawsuits had shut Hollywood's doors in our collective faces, and my attempt to smooth over the lingering bad feelings in Cannes had gone belly-up with the theft of my collection. When I phoned Luke back about a month or so later to say I'd decided to design the jewelry for Eva Elain, he didn't ask a single question about it. He took charge of the negotiations with the studio, but he must have wondered. After my father's lawsuits and the calamity in Cannes, movie stars wearing loaned Thorne & Company jewelry must have seemed like a very bad idea to him.

Still, none of it explains why Jerome was with him at my father's house. Except, of course, that it does. They must be looking for me. But together? It isn't anything I'd expect of Luke. He's always been my rock, my most stalwart champion, my dearest friend. And despite his disappointment that I'd let Mr. One-of-a-Kind go, it isn't like him to interfere in my personal life.

Maybe there's something wrong with the jewelry for tomorrow's party. I deliberately delayed the second set of pieces for the actual Oscar ceremony so that nothing could overshadow my leopard motifs. The other suite is set to be delivered later, not that it'll matter after what I've planned. I can understand Luke being perturbed by the delay, going to the workroom to check on the pieces, and then heading up to the house to see if I was staying there so he could ask me about it.

But Jerome? He's not supposed to be here at all. He's supposed to be in London.

I sip my sugary tea, trying to come up with a reason that makes any sense.

Is it possible that Luke is playing Cupid and called Jerome to Los Angeles? He told me about the invitation to the party. As the company's lead designer, the studio wants me to attend, but I said I wasn't sure I was up for public scrutiny and preferred that my pieces speak for themselves. I went on to say that Luke should go to represent us. I know how much he likes to get dressed up and flirt his way through a crowd. But after his chastisement, I also know how much he likes Jerome and what a mistake he thinks I made. Only, I've always had the feeling that he would secretly prefer it if I remained single like he is. Both of us devoted to the company because we work so well together. While Luke revered my father, Virgil

Thorne was never easy to work with. Luke had to swallow a lot of tirades and tantrums when my father was in charge because Virgil is an *artist* and behaved as he believed an artist should. I never followed his example in that regard. I'm an artist, too, but I quickly learned there's no place for artistic indulgence in business. My father taught me many things, and that was one of them, though he failed to follow his example in the end: Never let your emotions get in the way of your reputation.

I run my finger around the cup's rim.

Luke and Jerome.

Jerome and Luke.

It's a litany in my head, unfinished lyrics that I keep hearing over and over as I examine all the possible scenarios for why those two men are in LA together. Two men who mean the world to me in different ways. Along with my father, it's the trio that makes up my world.

And I have unfinished business with each of them.

With Luke because he doesn't know that my father betrayed us both by being the Leopard. With Jerome because I dragged him into this and let our feelings for each other burn too hotly. And with my father, because he turned against me, upending everything in my life and putting me in the terrible position of having to trap him to get my life back.

Jerome and Luke.

Luke and Jerome.

I leave the toast—no way I'm going to eat a slice—and go to the bedroom. The king-size bed is so inviting. And I'm so tired. So tired of thinking. Of planning and scheming. So tired of living like a thief. I just want it over with.

First, finish unpacking. Then a bath and try to get some sleep. Tomorrow is going to be a long day. I take the wig out of my bag and shake it. Once I put it over my straight, blond hair, I'll be a perky brunette. Then I remove the black capri pants and round-neck black jersey. Along with the catering apron and cap, I'll disappear into the staff serving the pre-Oscar guests, invisible in the way the help always is at these grandiose events, offering trays of hors d'oeuvres or flutes of champagne. Just another waitress among many.

Relieved that I actually have everything I need for tomorrow night, I let out a long breath. I think I have every angle covered. Every contingency taken into account. Or, at least, I did until tonight. I'd prepared for everything but this: having to flee the house and run from two of the three most important men in my life.

Luke and Jerome.

Jerome and Luke.

What was Luke thinking bringing my ex to my father's house at nine-thirty at night? Does he suspect something? Did I let something slip inadvertently? I've tried my utmost to keep him out of what I'm doing. Putting him in the middle of this would divide his loyalties. He's running the company for me. He's my father's longtime associate and friend. Outside the office, they always got along well, sharing the same taste in fine dining, the Met, and literature.

Unless Jerome went looking for Luke after he wouldn't take his calls and found out he was coming here. He's an investigator, after all. If he did and then told Luke what he knows about my father, that would be enough for Luke to help him...

My mind reels with the possibilities and potential disasters of their alliance. Forget the bath. I just want bed. I get undressed, dropping my slacks and sweater onto the settee, and then crawl between the sheets. I lay my head on the soft, down pillows. The Beverly Hills Hotel spares no expense; everything is perfection from the lightly scented air to the thick, plush carpet to the blackout shades to keep out the morning light. But not even the luxurious bed and heavenly pillows comfort me. My head is filled with thoughts of Jerome, ricocheting me from anger to desire. From the thrill of seeing him unfold himself from the car and stride after Luke to the fury of having him interrupt my so-meticulously-planned revenge. I've made sure not to repeat the mistakes from Venice and set the trap in such a way that my father can't help but be lured by it. This time, I want him to do what he does best. I want him to steal the loot. Because when he does, I'll be waiting for him up in his tree.

I designed the suite of jewelry for him.

But now, Jerome is here, throwing my plan into disarray. What is it about him that I just can't shake? What stops me from moving on? He's not that good-looking. Not at all suave. Not intellectual in the least. He certainly isn't the kind of man I ever envisioned falling in love with. Why can't I look at him without feeling the clench in my stomach and the sharp quickening of my breath? Why can't I let go of the memory of how it felt to be in his arms, skin against skin with him whispering in my ear? Not poetry but candid truths that are now seared in my heart, things I keep hearing over and over. Especially something he said to me as I lay falling asleep in Venice a year ago when we didn't know what would happen to us.

"I just want to lose myself in you, in your smell and taste. For a helluva long time. Maybe for all time."

I had wanted it, too, though I'd never told him.

And what's even worse? I still do.

Chapter Seven

Jerome

Quite the spread. I know Ania's family has a lot of money, on both sides, but this—it's something else. Not my idea of a home, too much glass everywhere makes me feel exposed. But the view is… Wow. From its perch over the canyon—how did they even manage to build a house that juts out over a cliff?—all of Los Angeles is spread out below, shimmering with lights. It really looks like the city of stars from way up here, a place where dreams are made.

Luke stands in the sunken living room, a little line pinching the skin between his eyebrows.

"What is it?" I ask. He'll have to orientate me; I don't know my way around.

"The housekeepers' car," he says, glancing about the living room as if he's searching for it in here.

"Yeah. What of it?" I step to the patio doors that look like they're part of the wall but slide open onto a quarry flagstone terrace with a low wire-railing wall at the end and a very nice pool. The rich live like the gods, and I've never cared. But this pool… I could get used to having something like this in my backyard. I used to swim competitively in college before signing up for the war. There's nothing like it to stay in shape, though with all my smoking, I'd probably swim four laps and drown.

"It's missing from the garage," Luke says from behind me.

"What?" I turn to see him moving to a kitchen surrounded by granite counters. The space is right off the living room, not tucked away as kitchens usually are. A dining area sits by it with a glass-topped table and eight plush, ivory-fabric-upholstered chairs, near an ebony bar with matching stools. The entire house feels futuristic to me, like it should belong on a spaceship.

"Is it important?" I see him opening and closing cabinets, checking the refrigerator.

"I don't know." His slight frown appears again. "It's the Millers'. But they went on vacation, so unless they took it and left it at the airport or it's in the cottage garage..."

"And the Millers would be?"

"The live-in help. Mr. Miller does the gardening, the pool maintenance, and such. Mrs. Miller sees to the house. I told you, it's rarely used anymore. Ania never came here often, and I don't think Virgil visited much anymore, either."

"Huh." I can tell he's perturbed. I take it as a good sign. "So, you think Ania is using the caretakers' car?"

"Maybe. Let's check the bedrooms."

Nothing jumps out at him as we search. Or me. The house has that slightly deserted feeling of a place where people rarely live. It could be a movie set. Except for the priceless modern art on the walls and the antique busts and sections of statues spot-lit on plinths like in a museum. A lot of expensive artwork here. I can tell because I started my insurance work investigating art stolen by the Nazis before moving into jewelry. If recovering stolen jewelry is a challenge, recovering stolen art is a feat. No wonder the Thornes keep full-time, live-in help.

"Do the Millers usually go on vacation and leave the place empty like this?"

Luke used an extra set of keys to gain entrance, and there's a pretty high gate and wall surrounding the front of the house. I didn't think anyone would scale the cliffside to steal anything, but still, it's a risk to just close an expensive place like this and go away.

"Their daughter lives in North Dakota," Luke replies. "They visit her every year, though I had no idea that anyone could possibly live in North Dakota."

I have to chuckle. He's such an inbred New Yorker. If it isn't New

York or Paris, it really shouldn't exist.

"Besides," he goes on, returning to the living room, "the house is secure, and they deserve a vacation, I suppose. They've been with the family for years, and a pool boy comes in while they're away."

"But no sign of Ania." I could use a cigarette. Seeing all this, the way she lives, the way she grew up, it hits me all over again—*way* out of my league. Like I could never keep up with this.

"No," he says as if relieved. "The refrigerator is empty, nothing in the cabinets except for some non-perishables. She's not staying here. I didn't think she would be."

We step out onto the pool terrace, where I light up.

"Let me have one of those," he says, surprising me.

"Sure." I extend my pack to him, and he grimaces. "Lucky Strikes?"

"Hey. I can't afford Dunhill."

He lights up and takes a deep inhale, doesn't even cough. Mr. Cologne must sneak a cigarette now and then on the side. It thaws me a little. The guy isn't so vice-free and perfect, after all.

"You might be able to afford it on your studio salary," he remarks, pacing to the lounge chairs by the pool. "You should afford it. This tastes like charred rope."

I stare past the pool to an almost indistinguishable building set back in the darkened garden grounds. "What's over there?"

"Nothing. The caretakers' cottage." He grinds out the barely smoked cigarette in an ashtray on a little poolside table. Guess he prefers Dunhill.

"Well?" I glance at him. "What about in there?"

He laughs. "Ania has the entire house at her disposal. Why on earth would she stay there? It's the Millers' residence. She'd never."

"Yeah. You never thought she'd turn into a thief like her father, either, did you?"

He goes still. Then he says, "Touché. Wait a second. I'll turn on the lights."

He flips a switch on the side of the house, and the entire flagstone path lights up like Christmas. Little glow lamps embedded in the ground toss shadows from the hibiscus bushes and palm trees and whatnot. Everything is immaculate but with an unkempt, lush, wild look in contrast to the house's stern angularity. It's a deliberate artifice that reminds me of Ania's designs for the studio: the classic elegance concealing the leopard by the clasp, ready to snap its fangs.

Luke leads me down the path and a short flight of stone steps. "It's probably locked," he says when we reach a cottage that's larger than any flat I've ever rented. Made of the same concrete and steel as the main house but with crimson bougainvillea vines growing all over it so it's practically hidden all the way here in the back. "I don't have an extra key. It's a private residence and—"

His voice cuts short as he tries the door, and it swings open.

"Now, that's odd…" he starts to say.

I push past him.

He flips on the lights. It's cozy and nicely furnished but not in the pristine, austere style of the house. Evidence of regular habitation appears in the clutter of framed photographs on the living room table, overladen bookshelves, faded pillows tossed on the sofa, and—

"A tuna sandwich." I pick it up off a plate on the kitchen counter. Sniff it. "Fresh, too."

Luke stares at me.

"The pool boy like tuna sandwiches?" I ask him.

Without a word, he darts into a hallway to a main bedroom. The bed is made, but he rips off the covers to finger the sheets. He looks up at me with a very troubled expression. "Bingo, Mr. Curtis. These are definitely not the Millers' bedsheets."

I almost scoff. But then he explains. "One of Ania's pet peeves is low thread count on her sheets. I'd have thought you knew that much by now. She only stays in five-star hotels because she must have high-thread-count sheets wherever she sleeps."

"And fresh flowers daily," I remark. "Like it really matters to her."

"Exactly. She is her father's daughter, after all. Only the best." Luke moves into the adjoining bathroom, pulling open drawers while I contemplate the disheveled bed.

She was sleeping right here. If I pick up one of those pillows, will it smell like her?

"Nothing in the bathroom." Luke emerges. "I feel awful, rummaging about like this."

"You're sure the sheets are proof that she…?"

"Of course, not. I'm not sure of anything where she's concerned anymore. But these sheets were brought from the main house. And who else would do it except Ania? Not the pool boy," he adds sarcastically. "I doubt he even knows what high thread counts are."

As he leaves the bedroom, he stumbles against a waste bin by a desk and scatters some garbage. He starts to retrieve it, and I leap forward, taking the balls of paper from him and rushing into the living room to spread them out under a lamp, smoothing the crinkles.

As I uncrumple them, Luke exhales sharply. "Those...those are sketches Ania made of the second suite for the Oscars ceremony. I recognize them. She changed some things at the last minute. She told me that was why the jewelry was delayed."

My heart starts to pound. I indicate the last paper, which isn't a sketch. It's indecipherable. To me, it looks like it might be an architectural plan of some kind with red Xs marking different spots.

"Any idea what this is?"

He peers at it. "None."

I nod, pocketing the papers. "Let's go."

On the drive back, which Luke does too fast, even though it's a steep, narrow road out of the canyon, neither of us speaks for a long time.

Eventually, he clears his throat. "She must have been there recently. She didn't put the regular sheets back and left her sketches in the trash. Not to mention the sandwich. She may have gone out but plans to return."

"No." I stare ahead at the road. "She's gone. Don't ask me how or why I know, but I do. Something spooked her, and she hightailed it out of there. Like she did in Venice."

He nods. "I'm very sorry about all of this."

"Why? You didn't do any of it."

"Yes, but..." He takes a curve too fast and has to hit the brakes. "She's been acting so peculiarly, and I never thought to insist that we meet up in person. Not even when I knew I was coming to LA and really should see her."

"I thought you two were best buddies."

"You don't understand." He takes a moment to collect his thoughts. "She's a very loyal friend, but she's not needy in that way. She grew up being told she had to be as dedicated and gifted as her father. He treated her like his sole heir, one he was grooming to take his throne. Yes, she had a very privileged life, but it was also very demanding. Virgil was completely oblivious to the fact that daughters need their fathers to tell them they're pretty. To let them go out on silly dates and attend high school dances. To make their own mistakes. After her mother passed away, it was just him and her, and he kept her under his constant control. She broke it off with Hugh Lockling of her own accord—a wise decision on her part—but she also did it because Virgil disliked him. He suspected Lockling's father had his eye on acquiring the company for their overstuffed portfolio. If Ania had married Hugh, they'd have eventually made him a shareholder in Thorne & Company. Virgil couldn't abide it. No man could ever take his place in his company or his daughter's heart."

"What a jerk. And he never told her she was pretty? She's drop-dead gorgeous."

"She is. But he only told her that she has a unique talent. That was more important than anything else. He molded her entire life. Pushed her hard to be the very best. But when it turned out that she actually was, I don't think he liked it."

"You can say that again." My hands clench in my lap. "He tried to ruin her career by stealing her collection in Cannes."

"He's jealous," says Luke quietly. "Envious of her success. I don't believe he wants to be. He was so proud of her when she joined the company to design under him. But her first pieces brought us a lot of new acclaim. She showed a more modern sensibility than he did. And he knew it. It's not easy for a king to have his only heir overthrow him."

"He's not a king. He's a fucking monster."

Luke steers us onto one of the city boulevards. "He is, but not by choice. Our business is extremely competitive. He had to make himself out of nothing. His family were Russian immigrants who fled their country. His father was a jeweler. Virgil built his company with hard work and—"

"Stealing from other companies," I cut in. "To cut out his competition and ruin them."

"Yes." Luke sighs. "I don't know him at all, it seems. He was doing it the entire time I worked for him. I remember the panic and fear running amok whenever the Leopard struck. Virgil always smiled and said, 'Not me. That thief won't dare come after my company or me.'"

"And they never did. Until Cannes."

"I still can't believe it." He turns onto Wilshire. "What are you going to do?"

"I don't know." I hate it. I loathe feeling so helpless. "She's definitely planning something, but I've no clue what. Those designs she made for the studio, hiding out in the caretakers' cottage, and hightailing it out of there are sure signs that, whatever it is, she's up to no good."

"Maybe the time has come for you to simply ask her," he says.

"How?" I turn to him. "She won't be going back to that house."

"At the pre-Oscar party. It's tomorrow night, remember?" He pulls up in front of my apartment building. "She was invited to attend. I asked her to come with me."

"And did she accept?" I growl, wondering why the hell he didn't tell me this before.

"No. She said the last thing she wanted was to abase herself at a Hollywood gala. She wants her pieces to shine and speak for themselves. But I'll certainly be there. As will you. You're escorting Eva Elain, guarding our jewelry at the party. Or am I wrong?"

"Yeah." I feel the papers in my jacket pocket. "I am." Not something I'm looking forward to, either, being a watchdog for the star. Or, as Luke might put it, her German shepherd.

"Ania may show up. She doesn't know you're here. I won't tell her, either, if she happens to try to reach me at my hotel. You can approach her at the party. She can't make a scene there."

"*If* she shows up."

"Jerome." He stops me as I reach for the door latch. "You have to speak to her. You have to tell her how you feel."

I freeze for a moment.

"She... I think she regrets it. What she did in Venice." Luke measures his tone. "She didn't sound at all like herself when she told me you'd split up. I could hear it in her voice. She's not needy, and she plays it very close to the vest, but I know her. She was miserable."

"Could have fooled me," I rasp. "She walked away and never looked back."

I yank open the door. As I step out, he says, "You're wrong. I believe she's never stopped looking back." I meet his eyes. "All of this, what's happening now, this is Ania, unable to keep from looking back. She's planning to get back at her father because of what he tried to do to you."

I don't have an answer for that. I'm not sure what to say, so all I say is, "Thanks for tonight. You went out of your way, and I won't forget it. If she does happen to call you, let me know right away. Don't let her think you suspect anything, though, okay? She's going to be on guard."

"Of course. Otherwise, I'll see you tomorrow." He gives me a weary smile and drives off.

I enter my building, where exhaustion falls upon me like a dead weight.

What are you doing, Ania? Where are you hiding?

The following day, I wake to find that Lauren has sent over my tuxedo for the party. It's in a garment bag outside my door. When I try it on, it's a near-perfect fit. A little snug in the crotch, but the pants break just where they should, and the matching, polished shoes are my size if a little too tight, as well. I look like a penguin in it, and I've no idea how to fasten a bow tie—it's the kind you have to knot, not clip on. I decide to forgo the ruffled tux shirt and wear my plain black shirt instead.

Black on black. Like my mood.

I drop my shirt off at the dry cleaner's and pay a fortune to have it back today, then drive my rented car to the Beverly Hills Hotel, a ridiculous, frothy pink building that looks like Mae West's hat. I have to walk the ballroom and make sure there are no security risks for tonight. I doubt there'll be anything to be concerned about at a fancy party with big celebrities in a swanky big-star hotel, but it's my job, and I have to keep busy. I need to keep my mind on my work and not on Ania.

She might show up tonight. If she does, what am I going to say to her?

The ballroom is gilded and overwrought like Mae West's saloon. There's an upper gallery where invited journalists will report on the stars and industry bigwigs mingling below for their tabloids. Hotel personnel set up cocktail tables, and maids vacuum the carpet. I check the exits and entrances, noting where each one goes. Then, as I look at my wristwatch and realize I only have a few hours to drive by the cleaner's to pick up my shirt, eat a quick lunch, shower, shave, and get dressed in my penguin suit to drive to the studio to retrieve my gun—the studio has me licensed to carry one—and meet Miss Elain—we're taking a studio limo to the party, of course—I reach for my cigarettes in my jacket and feel the papers I stashed there last night.

I never removed them. I'd fallen into bed in my shorts, so tired that I passed out. Now, as I pull out the one with the strange markings, my blood turns to ice.

It's a floorplan, all right. Of this very ballroom. Every exit and entrance I just noted is marked by a red X. Ania drew up the plan, with all the ways in and out.

She's planning something for tonight. At the party.

I can barely keep myself together as I speed like a maniac to get my shirt and return to my apartment. I gulp down a bowl of cold cereal for lunch, hop in the shower and shave too close, nicking my chin, then throw on my tuxedo and stuff the bow tie into my pocket. Someone will have to help me tie it. Maybe Lauren if I see her at the studio. If not, whatever.

I'll go to the party with my shirt collar open like the slob I am.

As I drive to the studio in the haze of a Los Angeles afternoon, all I can think about is her.

Will she be at the party tonight? And how will I react if I discover that she's planning another heist to ensnare her father, right under my nose?

Chapter Eight

Ania

When I was a little girl, I used to spy on my parents' cocktail parties from behind the living room drapes. I'd be in my pink nightgown with its lace ruffles, fuzzy slippers on my feet, and they'd be in their evening clothes, the women in dazzling jewelry—everyone always wore their best to a fête at the Thorne penthouse.

The evenings always started sedately, but after the first hour or so, the guests plied with champagne or something stronger, my entertainment would begin. This guest flirting with that one; two men squaring off over a political dispute; a group of women gossiping about another across the room, oblivious to their tattle.

The longer the party went on, the more intense it became. The flirting became more brazen, the arguments more heated. The jokes turned bawdier, and the barbs nastier. I noticed everything and filed it away in an effort to understand something about grownups, who were still quite mysterious to me. *So this is how adults have fun*, I thought.

Now, all these years later, I'm standing behind similar, if metaphorical, drapes. Instead of my nightgown, I'm in a catering outfit—black pants and top, apron and cap—holding a silver tray of cheese puffs and watching the grownups drink and flirt.

At my parents' parties, I never tired of waiting for the bad behavior to start. It always did. And it will here tonight, as well. The big difference being that the bad behavior tonight will have been instigated by me, and

I'm sick over it. I've planned and plotted this night for months, but now that it's upon me, how can I be sure if it's what I really want? The end of this evening—of this heist if it happens—will conclude a part of my life that I never imagined I'd have to go through.

I didn't think tonight would be as difficult to endure as it's turning out to be. I don't even know which part of it is the worst: that I'm setting up my father to expose himself and force a confrontation that will most likely end our relationship—or that I want it. *Is* that what I really want? Revenge, yes. Maybe repentance, too. But the finality of permanent estrangement?

Or is it that Luke will inevitably be drawn into this mess and find himself in a position where he has to confront what his friend and longtime employer is made of, the very man who hired and promoted him?

Or is it that I'm risking the reputation of Thorne & Company should anything go wrong?

The mix of so many different perfumes and colognes in the air makes me slightly nauseous. I've never been this sensitive to scents at events before. Is it just my nerves making me sick to my stomach? Either is possible. The latter more probable.

I take a tentative step into the crowd, tray out in front of me, offering my wares. I'm on the lookout for my father. The studio extended the invitation to him, as well, and he's never been one to eschew flattery. The importance of the evening—our house designing jewelry expressly for the top-nominated female star of this year's Oscars show, regardless of whether she wins the gold statuette or not—should be too tempting for him to stay away.

He'll probably feel safe enough to come, too. He's never been a regular face in the news, or at least he wasn't for most of his career until he started suing Hollywood. But that's all come and gone by now. Mostly, he managed to remain the enigmatic jeweler known only to his clients and not the press or gossip columnists. He practiced discretion as an integral part of our business. I can still remember him telling me, *"Ania, don't ever let our pieces be overshadowed by us. We are only the hands that create them."*

The memory tightens my throat as I think of how he was also the hands that stole the jewelry. Still, no one here knows that. And no one will be expecting him, either, as he's officially retired from the company. It would be just like him to appear to test the mood. Having been ousted for suing some of the most famous stars because they wouldn't return pieces he'd loaned to them, those who know who he is will be outraged to see him at one of the most important celebrations on Hollywood's calendar. He'll delight in it, revel in the sideways glances and clenched-teeth greetings. He'll even pause to admire any Thorne pieces that others may be wearing, remarking on how he recalls how they were created. He has a memory like an elephant; it's one of the qualities that I was most in awe of. My father never forgets a detail.

The memory of an elephant and the stealth of a cat. You need both to be a master thief.

He'd better show up.

Even if part of me hopes he doesn't.

I'm so torn. Have been for so long that it's become my natural state of being. I need him to sneak in and steal our jewelry so I can follow him and find where he's stashed the rest of it and steal that from *him*, finally righting the wrongs he's done. Clean the slate for myself and my business. What I'll do after that—give up Thorne & Company, stay with it and move forward, or retire myself and let someone else take over—is up for grabs. All I know is that those pieces he took, which have never been seen again or sold on the black market, must be returned. I won't rest easy until they are. He took a life in London, that poor jeweler's assistant who came upon him unexpectedly, and ruined many others. I can't atone for any of that, but I *can* see that the jewels he took are returned to their rightful owners. I can't figure out my life or my future until that's done.

At the same time, I desperately *don't* want him to come here tonight. I don't want to chase him to his lair. I don't want to face him, his duplicity and thievery. I want my past back, my innocence. I want to be my father's loving daughter again.

As I work my way through the crowd, my tray emptying, I'm grateful for my server disguise. I'm anonymous. No one pays me any attention as they pluck the cheesy hors d'oeuvres off the tray. I'm invisible to them and will be to my father, as well. Once you've lived in the rarefied upper crust of society, you are locked into its mores. You never see the help unless they spill wine on you. I'll be able to track my father without anyone noticing.

The ballroom has a hum of low-grade anxiety. The star of the night, Eva Elain, hasn't yet appeared, and the party can't take off until she does. I'm curious myself. It'll be my first time seeing her wearing the pieces I designed for her. It occurs to me that the studio might have hired a security goon to stick by her to protect the jewelry, given its value. Virgil will have to get around him if there's a bodyguard with her. For anyone else, that wouldn't be easy. But my father has proven so many times that nothing impedes him. Bodyguard or not, he'll figure a way. To date, no one's deciphered how the Leopard accomplished his daring feats. Including me. He taught me everything he knew. Except, it seems, how to disappear after stealing millions of dollars in jewels.

After another thirty minutes or so and another tray of hors d'oeuvres I have to covertly swipe from the catering area while the other waiters are circulating, excitement ripples through the crowd.

Eva Elain has arrived. It's been a long time coming for her. She toiled in a slate of B films for years, along with enduring two failed marriages and, if the tabloids are to be believed, a car accident with husband number two that led to a miscarriage. All in sacrifice to her pursuit of fame. Now, she's reached it with a picture that's really nothing special: an implausible, long-winded African epic where she plays a nineteenth-century heiress tracking down her long-lost husband, with the expected native perils and hidden treasure, but with spectacular on-site locations in Kenya, and a performance that every critic hailed as her best. There's practically no chance that she won't win the award for best actress. Even if her competition is stiff, none of the other nominees have her particular brand of pathos, her single-minded grit, or Segal Pictures' full-blown resources to back her up. She's the queen of the marquee, her picture the highest grossing of the year—at least, for the time being. Queens don't last long in Hollywood.

The lights in the room dim. I took this into account in my designs. Spotlights trained on her as she makes her long-awaited—and no doubt intentionally delayed—entrance. I sourced exceptionally fine-faceted stones for my pieces, so they would shimmer and dazzle as befitting their wearer.

Like everyone else in the room, my eyes are on the doors as they swing open, and the guest of honor enters. My design paid off. Eva Elain is glittering and—

I no longer see her. Am no longer aware of my yellow diamonds and emeralds or the crowd gasping in unison. I don't hear anything except the pounding of my heartbeat, too loud in my ears.

How am I not prepared? I should have realized it when I saw him at my father's house with Luke. Should have recalled how chatty he'd been with Lauren Segal in Venice. Damn her. She's been after him since she first met him at Julie Kimbell's masquerade, and I bet she now thinks she has him. A studio job in Hollywood after he got dumped by his ice-queen lady friend. I should have my head examined for not putting it all together beforehand so that instead of being shocked while holding a tray of pigs-in-blankets, I'd be braced to see him.

How could I not have realized that he'd be who the studio hired to protect my jewelry? And he must know it's mine. That's why he came to the house. Luke arrived in LA to deliver the jewelry and took pity on him. Agreed to help him track me down. Jerome had been with Luke last night, searching for me, so he could look me in the face and ask why I left him in Venice without an explanation—though I'd thought the fake Lemon Twist would be explanation enough.

My first instinct is to hand my tray to anyone nearby—guest or waiter—and make a run for it. But I can't. Too much depends on this. Too many months of planning. Too much rests on my ability to bring an end to this nightmare, once and for all.

I can't stop watching as Eva, Jerome following a few paces behind in a well-fitted tux sans bow tie, makes her way into the ballroom, greeted by a sudden, too-exuberant round of applause. Eva smiles and nods and soaks in every second of the attention. Jerome just looks uncomfortable, a slight frown on his face. He must hate all this.

He's a wrench in my plans that I didn't account for. I'm no longer sure I can even carry it out if he's guarding the jewels. What will he do if he notices me? Will he try to stop me? Or will he let it go far enough to see where it leads? Unlike any hired gun on the lookout for trouble, Jerome will know exactly what trouble there might be. He'll know who he must stop and what the modus operandi is. He isn't a security guard; he's an insider. He's never met Virgil in person, but he has as much at stake as I do. He put himself on the line to help me, and my father went after him. If the Leopard shows up, Jerome won't let him pounce. And that makes the situation too unpredictable for my liking.

Lauren Segal approaches Eva with a flute of champagne. Nothing for Jerome, of course—he's on duty—but she does give him a quick look. An intimate one, as if she owns him. She puts her hand on his arm and whispers to him. Logic tells me it must be about the event, directives for the evening, but I don't feel logical about this. I want to storm over there and claim him as mine.

Except this is the very last place where I can afford to make a scene. I won't blow up all my efforts over a man. Even this man…

Oh, this man. I hate how weak my heart is, how feeble my willpower is when it comes to him. He just walks into a room and turns my entire being inside out.

And then, before I'm barely used to the shock, the next one arrives. This time, I'm not too surprised. I did expect it, after all. I planned for it. Set everything up for this moment. I invited him as much as the studio did. And yet, it undoes me all the same.

He enters unnoticed in a tux like every other man here. He's sporting a beard and black-rimmed glasses, so I'm not sure at first. He continues farther into the room without anyone approaching him. He doesn't stop to chat with anyone, either, like he's a random stranger here to witness the festivities. Reaching a waiter with a tray of champagne, he takes one of the flutes.

The lights illuminate the jewelry in the ballroom, shining off precious metals and gemstone surfaces, glinting off the ring on his index finger as he sips from the flute. I suck in a breath. No one else will recognize it, but I do. It's my father's signature ring.

I look back at Jerome. I was wrong.

One other person will know who this man is if they see him.

And it's the very last person in the world I want to know.

Chapter Nine

Jerome

I've never much liked going to parties. The noise, the excuse to overdrink, the loose tongues and regrets later. Eva is caught up in her moment of supremacy, however, posing as if camera bulbs are flashing, accepting the homage as if she's already won the main event.

I suppose she probably will. A lot of fuss for a silly statuette, but what do I know about these things? A few days ago, before everything started to turn sideways, Lauren and I grabbed coffee and cigarettes on the studio lot, where she told me that the studio's pre-Oscar gala—she actually used the word *gala*—is unprecedented. No studio wastes the money to boost their nominated star's PR picture the night before the ceremony unless it's a poster on a main boulevard.

"Why not?" I asked.

"The Academy's already voted," she said. "No point."

"Then…?"

"Why are we doing it? Because they're our first nominations, and my father says that no matter if we win or lose, if we throw a party to celebrate it, we're winners." Lauren shrugged. "And he wants to keep Eva happy. We've got another script for her, but she's delayed signing on to see if she wins."

"Holding out for a better offer?"

"Better money," she harrumphed.

Eva's certainly the toast of the money now. She's not a bad sort, for an actress.

When we met at the studio, Lauren had already left for the hotel, and Eva was running late, of course, finishing having her makeup applied, so I loitered outside by the limo until she appeared.

She ignored Luke's advice and opted for a very low-cut, gold, pleated number that might have muted the jewels except that nothing except a potato sack thrown over them could mute Ania's exquisite work, and Eva Elain's bared and unblemished shoulders were definitely not a potato sack. Once in the car, she gave me a very wide, red-lipped smile and said, "Light me up a cigarette, will you? I'm dying for a hit."

I did, rolling down the window to let the smoke out as she puffed and gazed with detached interest at the passing city.

"Big night, huh?" I said, trying to make idle conversation. For some reason, I was nervous. Or for a very specific reason that had nothing to do with why she likely was.

"Yes." Her red-lipped mouth grimaced. "The baubles look all right?"

The jewels encircled her skin like the feline creations they were.

"Yeah. Very nice," I remarked.

"And very expensive." She crushed out her cigarette in the rear-seat-compartment ashtray. "Worth more than me, I'll bet. And a lot more than what I got paid for that lousy picture everyone seems to think is the cat's meow. Have you ever been to Africa?"

"Can't say that I have."

"A hellhole. Bugs everywhere. The stinging kind. And spiders. Filming on location was hell, too. I was in a corset for the first half of the shoot. A corset. In Africa. In a thousand-degree heat."

It seemed to me that she was also in one now given her choice of dress.

"Then I get nominated for it. For surviving malaria, a stampede of supposedly trained rhinos that trampled over the set, and my co-star making a pass at me every damn chance he got as if I would ever sleep with Hollywood's most notorious adulterer. Never mind the gossip columnists. He might have crabs, considering where he puts his dick."

I had to smile. She wasn't a star behind closed doors—the mouth on her.

"But the director didn't make a pass?" I said, meaning it as a feeble joke.

"He might have, but not at me. The director is a fairy. Like your very well-groomed friend from Thorne & Company." She let out a sigh. "The best ones always are."

"I'm not," I said, for no reason and too defensively, which was utterly ridiculous. I'd never cared where anyone put their dick, as she described it, so long as no one got hurt and everyone was of consenting age and actually consented.

"I didn't think you were. Tell me about yourself. Traffic at this hour…who knows when we'll get there. Better late than never."

I relayed the minimal details: my time in the Army during the war, then my decision to stay in Europe, and my investigative work in London—of which I said barely anything. I'd thought it would make me uncomfortable. I'd never enjoyed talking about myself, but Eva could make someone feel as if her sole interest was them. As if whatever someone told her was totally fascinating. Unlike Ania, who didn't bother to disguise her impatience whenever she was bored.

Yeah, Eva was still an actress behind closed doors. Though it wasn't like I was delivering a serenade.

"And from dreary London to star-spangled LA." She smoothed her red-lacquered, long-nailed hands over the pleats of her dress, her index finger adorned with the Thorne emerald. "Liking it?"

"I suppose it's okay if you like this sort of thing."

She chuckled. "That's about the extent of it. Gotta like this sort of thing, or you'll never make it in this town. Hey." She eyed me. "Planning on wearing a necktie to the party?"

I fished the crumpled article out of my pocket. "I don't know how to tie it."

"Don't look at me." She wiggled her fingers. "Fresh manicure. I'm not going to break a nail."

This time, I laughed. Like I said, she wasn't a bad sort.

Once we reached the hotel, she said, "I know we both have jobs to do tonight. But just do me a favor, okay? Don't step on my dress, and don't follow me around like I'm going to make off with all this priceless loot on me. The tabloids are relentless. They see you at my heels, and within ten seconds, they'll be printing front-page headlines about how Miss Elain was seen out on the town on the eve of her surefire Oscar win with a very mysterious and handsome stranger." She paused, fixing her stare on me. "Interested in being the very mysterious and handsome stranger?"

"Hell, no."

"I didn't think so." She shimmied out of the car as the driver held open the rear door.

Now she's drinking down champagne and drinking in the applause. Lauren sidles up to me to whisper, "Keep an eye on her, but let her show off. She can work a crowd like a pro."

"Still hasn't signed that offer, has she?" I ask dryly.

Lauren elbows me. "Not yet. But after what we spent on this party, she'd better."

I'll have a tough time keeping track of Eva if she starts flittering about, but I'm not worried about that. I have my eye on someone else entirely, and as the lights go up a bit, not too much—why ruin the illusion of eternal youth in Hollywood?—I scan the ballroom to see if I catch sight of Ania. Impossible to tell. Too many people, and there's the upper gallery, which isn't well-lit at all. She could be anywhere. Or nowhere.

Lauren goes to do her rounds as the studio publicist. I feel like a third wheel, my gun holstered under my jacket, no necktie, no drinking tonight because I'm on the job, and not much to do. I keep staring at overdressed people as they walk by and receive a few appreciative glances in return, the covert wish-I-could-ask-for-your-number kind, from women mostly, but a few guys give me the look, too.

The mysterious, handsome stranger. What the hell am I doing here?

I'm relieved when Luke wades his way through the crowd to me. He's picture-perfect in a dark blue tuxedo, classic cut but with a touch of flair in its color. He looks as if he was born in a tux.

"No bow tie?" he remarks. "How *Rebel Without a Cause* of you."

"I don't know how to tie the damn thing," I snap.

"Well. I'd offer to do it for you, but…" He arches an eyebrow.

"Forget it, pal," I say, but I'm glad to see him. Someone to talk to so I'm not standing around like a German shepherd while Eva gets applauded at every table she happens to wander to.

Instead, I tell Luke what I discovered about the sketch. "She scouted out this ballroom in advance, which means she plans on something happening here. Have you seen her yet?"

He shakes his head. "I've been looking for her. I left a message at our office in New York in case she calls in. Don't worry. I made it sound like I was reminding her that I'd escort her to the party if she decided to come and wanted to make sure the second suite would be delivered first thing tomorrow morning. Not that it matters." He looks at Eva, laughing off some compliment as she moves on, working the crowd like a pro. "That's not the dress I told Miss Elain was best for the jewels, so she can choose whatever she prefers for the ceremony."

"Forget the dress. Did Ania call in to the office?"

"She did not. She also didn't show up in the workroom. I checked there, too, just in case. I'm afraid you were right. She...how did you put it again? Hightailed it out of Los Angeles."

As he surveys the crowd with an air that tells me he's not having much fun either, he suddenly goes still as if frozen in place.

I follow his stare across the ballroom where people are grouping at tables for a light catered dinner now that the star has made her appearance. I glimpse a tall, bearded man walking toward us.

Luke hisses. "My God, the nerve of him. In the very flesh."

I go cold. "What?"

"Virgil Thorne," Luke spits out. "The studio invited him as a matter of course, and I sent on the invitation, but I didn't think he'd ever..." He sets down his champagne flute with a hard clink of glass that I can clearly hear. "I can't do this now. Not here. I'm liable to punch him."

Mr. Cologne has a temper. Who knew?

"Don't react," I start to warn him, but the man is almost upon us, a strange half-smile on his face, and Luke turns white as a ghost.

I've never seen Virgil Thorne in person. He's a big man. Broad shouldered and very fit. I expected the fit part; you'd have to be to steal the kind of loot he has. But not the size. Ania is small-boned, not short for a woman but built like a ballerina so that all those arugula salads with a teaspoon of goose pâté isn't what she should be eating. She needs a regular diet of burgers.

On the other hand, her father looks as if he eats his meat raw. As the chilling metaphor slices through me, he turns to Luke and says in a polished tone, "My friend, how nice to see you again. I must apologize for my unacceptable tardiness."

"For...for what?" Luke might be as suave as a man can be, even when faced with an indecisive movie star or a car chase in Paris, but right now, he's having trouble stringing two words together.

"For not returning your calls in New York. You invited me to dinner and the opera. I'm sorry I never answered you, but I've been abroad." As Virgil says this, he meets my stare.

Blue eyes like Ania's but not her mercurial icy or grayish hue. His are a dark blue bordering on black and almost flat like a predator's. He directs his words at me.

"No reason to apologize," Luke says, mustering his manners. "My offer stands whenever you have the spare time, Virgil."

"Of course. Luke, we do need to catch up, but if you'll please excuse us for a moment, I have something important to discuss with Mr. Curtis." Virgil doesn't take his eyes from me as Luke hesitates as if he's not sure what to do. I nod, not looking away either, and Luke says in a low, terse voice to Virgil before walking off, "I'm ashamed of you."

Suddenly, I'm alone with the man who nearly got Luke killed in Paris, who stole from his daughter in Cannes, and set me up in Venice. At long last, face-to-face.

Just me and the Leopard.

His smile widens. It's not a nice one at all. "You told him."

"I did." My hand itches to yank out my gun. But I can't start pointing a weapon and yelling for his arrest. He's done nothing illegal here, and I have no evidence. If I accuse Virgil Thorne at the studio party of being the thief who's eluded capture for years, I'm the one who's liable to get arrested.

I want to do it anyway. Bring his house of lies crashing down on his head in the very town where he sowed his destruction as Thorne & Company's CEO.

"So," I say instead. "If you're thinking of doing anything to Ania, better think again because you'll have to go through me. And Luke. He really wants to sock you in the jaw right about now."

His smile doesn't waver. "You've turned my most trusted associate, a man I personally hired and trained and then later befriended, against me. You seduced my daughter and turned her against me, too. Oh, Mr. Curtis. If I plan to go through you, you won't even know it until it's over, as I did in Venice. And this time, your little studio redhead won't be able to spring you out of it."

In that moment, I understand. He's taken Ania's bait. He's here to steal her new jewelry. He's not going to get away with it. Not again. I'm going to make damn sure he doesn't get away with it.

"Just try me." I level my gaze with his flat blue eyes.

He steps back without another word. And though I watch him move away, step-by-step, it's as if he's melting into the crowd. As if he was never here at all. He disappears within seconds.

My body pulses with adrenaline. I tell myself to go after him. But he won't steal the jewels off Eva's neck. The Leopard never steals in that over-the-top manner, no matter how the movies like to depict it. He'll wait until the jewelry is returned for safekeeping, and then he'll make his move. In quiet, with the time he needs to get the loot and get away.

The safekeeping tonight is me.

I plunge into the party to search for Luke, finding him at the bar downing a whiskey. I can relate; I could really use one myself.

"I can't believe it," he bursts out. "He—he dares to show his face here after what he's done? As if nothing at all is wrong. As if—"

I seize him by the arm. "Forget it. Listen to me. He's here to steal the jewelry. I told you, Ania invited him with her designs. Their game isn't over, not by a long shot, so we need to end it. Now."

"How?" His question is stone-cold. I've seen how he can shrug off even a car accident after stuffing Ania's shoes in jewelry cases to confuse the thief. He can be very cool under pressure.

"We're taking the jewelry someplace where we can catch him. You have the safety codes to the case, right? I have to lock up the pieces with you to secure them."

"Yes." He taps his temple. "I keep the codes right here."

"We're going to catch that sonofabitch. And the only way to do it is to get the jewelry away before he has a chance to steal it. Let him come after us."

We have to wait until the party winds down. I can't just march up to Eva and demand that she return the jewelry before it's time. But as soon as the dinner ends—I can't eat a bite, sick to my stomach as I find myself scanning every corner, every table, hoping against hope to find Ania among the guests, pretending she doesn't see me so I can warn her before it's too late, though this is exactly what she must have planned—people start to say goodbye, retrieving their fur wraps and coats, air-kissing each other with good luck wishes for the Oscar ceremony.

Eva is chatting up a storm at the table reserved for her and her fellow cast members, one of whom is pounding down whiskey and giving her a sodden look, up and down. Must be the co-star, Hollywood's most notorious adulterer with the indiscriminate dick.

At my approach, Eva glances up. I can tell by her expression that she's not pleased.

"I'm not ready to leave," she informs me.

"You don't have to," I say. "Stay as long as you like. Can I speak to you in private, though? It won't take but a minute. Promise."

She reluctantly follows me into the side room off the ballroom, which Luke and I scouted out earlier. As soon as we're inside, Luke shuts the door and plants himself before it.

"What the hell is this?" Eva's voice rises. Oh, yeah. She's always an actress, no matter what. Can activate the histrionics on cue, at the mere closure of a door.

"Party's over," I tell her. "Time to put the Thorne diamonds to bed."

"Absolutely, not." She raises her hand to the necklace. "I'm not leaving this hotel without my jewelry. Are you insane? There are photographers outside, waiting for me—"

Her voice cuts off as Luke moves behind her. With a deft flick of his fingers, he unclasps the necklace and drops it neatly into his other hand. Then he reaches around her waist and removes the ring from her finger before she can react.

Eva gasps.

"I am sorry," Luke says, as if he truly means it. "But this isn't your jewelry, Miss Elain."

"I—what am I *supposed* to do?" she shrieks as Luke locks the jewelry in the case.

We move to the door. Luke pauses to glance over his shoulder at her. "I did advise you to wear the Dior. It was so perfect, with the most exquisite line. If you had, the photographers would never notice the missing jewelry in the heat of your departure. I do know how to dress, Miss Elain. That Marilyn Monroe getup was hardly the right choice for you."

She gapes at us, dumbfounded.

Racing to the parking garage, we jump into Luke's white Cadillac.

"Where to?" he asks, pulling out of the hotel at his usual reckless speed, evading the crush of departing automobiles by taking a private side exit.

"The Thorne house," I say without hesitation. "If Virgil was watching us—and I'm pretty sure he was—he'll follow."

"And then what?" He sounds much more like himself.

"Time to end this." I open my jacket and unholster my gun.

Chapter Ten

Ania

Everything that could possibly go wrong has gone wrong tonight, except for the jewelry falling apart. I almost wish the stones *had* fallen out of their settings. It would have precluded what's happening now. The tray of hors d'oeuvres feels too heavy, and I shift it in my hands, taking a few steps to the right to get a better look into the ballroom.

"Are those cheese or salmon?" asks an older woman, her pudgy fingers hovering over my neglected tray. "I'm very allergic to salmon. I can't even eat something that's next to salmon."

"These are most definitely salmon," I snap at her.

She recoils from me. I don't care. The upper gallery is for journalists and reporters, and they've been eating up all the canapes like it's their last meal.

I resume my search below. Months of planning to the exclusion of everything else in my life, driven by revenge and the need for resolution. To putting a stop to my father's spree forever. I yearn for a reckoning. I want it so desperately that I gave up a relationship with the first man I've ever loved, truly loved, for it.

And here's the man, about to ruin my plan.

Damn you, Jerome. You just have to go and be the hero, don't you? Have to take control. Have to handle the situation.

The very reasons I'm so attracted to him are why I'm furious with him now.

I watch the crowd, seeing my father approaching my ex-lover, whom he tried to set up in Venice. Even from up here in the gallery, I can see Jerome's reaction, and it gives me chills. This is a nightmare beyond anything I could have imagined. But, truth be told, I didn't spend any of the last year imagining what might go wrong, at least not as far as Jerome was concerned. I planned for how to make everything go right. That's the difference between me and my father, the man who always anticipated every contingency while creating a piece of jewelry and, I assume, plotting a heist. I see only the best that could happen. He dwells on potential flaws. After he killed that jeweler's assistant in London, he must have learned that flaws were inevitable in his chosen line of crime. And no amount of lecturing on why I must think about the negatives as well as the positives changed my methods. I was entirely my mother's daughter in that regard. And it appears it's about to be my undoing, one way or the other.

Jerome stares at my father. Would his face be this easy for anyone to read or is it just that his expressions are ingrained in my mind? I've memorized his every nuance. In my head, I can hear his voice, gruff, bordering on sarcastic, telling me exactly how *not* all right this situation is.

My father says something to Jerome.

I wish I knew what he said because Jerome's eyes narrow, and his jaw tightens. Then my father turns and walks away. Jerome looks as if he might go after him. I see his entire posture go rigid, but then he turns to search the crowd. Who is he looking for? I see him move toward the bar, which is located under the gallery, and I want to yell at him not to take his eyes off my father. But he wouldn't hear me. Even if he did, he probably wouldn't listen. He's seen the flaws, too, the scandal he'll cause if he raises a stink here at the party. He's letting my father go—for now. I watch helplessly as my father melts into the crowd, moving in the opposite direction. Seconds later, he disappears. Like a magic act. Like a leopard leaping up into its tree.

It seems like hours pass before dinner is served, though it's less than thirty minutes, and I see Jerome taking his seat at a table with Lauren Segal and others. I notice from my hiding spot in the gallery that he doesn't glance at his plate, but he has to wait out the meal for whatever he's planning to do next. I take advantage of the lull to bolt into the upstairs bathroom and divest myself of my catering accessories, tossing the apron, wig, and cap into the trash. I managed to elude any questions while circulating trays of canapes, but I'm not hired staff. I can't risk serving the dinner. When I return to the near-empty gallery, my black outfit concealing me, Jerome is speaking to Eva. He's saying something that she doesn't appear happy about. She shakes her head.

A man approaches me. "Do you have any more champagne…?"

"Can't you see I'm off-duty?" I return his bleary stare. He's had too much to drink, and at this point, what more can happen? It's unlikely anyone will recognize me in my slim black outfit, my hair slicked back into a bun, no makeup or accessories.

The man blunders off, muttering about the rude hired help.

I return my attention to Jerome. Judging by his body language, he's insisting that Eva comply. She rises to her feet, and he escorts her to a doorway.

Where is my father? Has he decided to abandon his plan after finding Jerome here? The tiny bubble of relief I feel can't overcome my growing despair. And loneliness. I'm up here by myself, watching my plan unravel below me. Caught up in this lunatic game of cat-and-mouse. Or rather, a lunatic game of leopard-and-rat. Because that's what I am, isn't it? A rat for abandoning my lover. For wanting to catch my father. For lying to Luke about what I'm doing.

I'm frozen here, waiting. It's suddenly become my default position.

Where did my father go?

Where did Jerome take Eva?

What should I do?

Before I can decide, Jerome leaves by the same door he entered with Eva. She's not with him, but Luke is. I can immediately tell that something is off. They're walking very fast. For a terrifying moment, I can't figure out what it could be. Then I wonder how I didn't see it immediately.

The jewels. Luke is carrying the case. They took my jewelry from Eva. Is my father waiting for them? Jerome wouldn't just give up and let my father steal it. The studio hired him to protect it, and that's exactly what he's going to do, even if it means a confrontation to the death.

Luke and Jerome hasten out of the ballroom. Eva emerges moments later with an enraged expression.

"Smart, Jerome," I whisper to myself in begrudging admiration.

"Make the Leopard chase after you."

And that's when it all clicks into place. I know exactly what he's doing.

Jerome has somehow figured out my plan and ripped it out from under me. He's taking the jewelry to draw my father to wherever he thinks he'll have the upper hand.

I race out of the gallery and down the stairs. I'm hoping enough people will be clamoring around Eva to delay Luke and Jerome so I can catch up.

Eva is in the lobby, mobbed by a crowd of well-wishers and flash-bulb-spitting photographers. I slink past her, out the front of the hotel. I didn't leave my car with the valet. I left the station wagon parked on the street. As I rush to it, a white Cadillac speeds past me.

The same car that Luke and Jerome went to the house in.

I follow, dodging them through the evening traffic, though a station wagon is hardly the best car to engage in a covert pursuit. If they're heading to the studio, I won't be able to follow them inside. But after about forty minutes, they make the turn onto the road to the canyon, and I know, with a sharp jolt in my stomach, where they're heading.

I have to slow down. The station wagon is protesting, plus I need to let enough cars get between us so they don't notice me trailing behind like a mad housewife. I don't know what kind of a trap he's hoping to set, but I can't let Jerome see me. I lose sight of them on the twisting canyon road and slow down again. Switch off my lights and risk driving in the pitch-dark because there's too little traffic here to conceal me.

When I see the house looming above on the cliff, the living room lights switch on. After parking down the hill and closing the car door as silently as I can, I sneak up. The living room window shines like a beacon, but the rest of the house is dark.

Now that I'm a few dozen yards away, I can see the locked jewelry case, clearly visible on the table in the window—as if they've put it on display. Using it as bait. I climb up the part of the wall by the caretakers' cottage, a hidden section that's lower than in the front of the house, not wanting to use my key on the side gate and make noise, then have to pause to take a much-needed breath.

I'm panting. I'm sneaking back into my family residence like…*like a thief*, I think, with the sudden urge to burst out laughing. Or sobbing.

Then I glimpse something moving ahead of me. Above me.

It could be a raccoon on the roof. Plenty of them in this area, especially at night. I watch and wait. The shadow enlarges, distorted by the light spilling out from the living room windows, and then I discern a man's figure, sliding down a rope to the pool terrace doors.

How can my father already be here? Ahead of me. Anticipating them.

Anxiety slams through me, cutting off my breath. I inch closer. As I step into the deep shadows by the pool, I spy Jerome lurking in the hallway just out of view of the terrace doors, the same direction my father will have to take to enter. For the second or the tenth or the hundredth time tonight, I can't move.

Jerome is holding a gun.

I have no doubt that if my father tries to steal that case, Jerome will shoot him point-blank if necessary. He won't think twice, not after Cannes and Venice.

Since I learned who and what my father is, all I've wanted is for him to answer for his crimes. Except I didn't really think through what that might actually entail. I've been so determined to confront him that I never considered the possibility that he might not want to be confronted by me again. That he might end up evading me. Or worse.

As the Leopard creeps to the terrace doors, I know I can't let Jerome shoot or possibly kill my father. Not only for my father's sake or mine, but for his. He'll carry my father's murder on his conscience for the rest of his life. More importantly, it will be splashed all over every newspaper, an international sensation: the crazed insurance investigator-turned-studio-security, so obsessed with finding the Leopard that he murdered Virgil Thorne in cold blood. He won't be able to convince the police that my father was a master thief, entering his own home to plunder his daughter's jewelry. He'll just sound insane, and they'll throw the book at him and lock him up in prison for the rest of his life. Even if I come forth to support his claim, who will believe us? We have no proof. No evidence. I never found my father's stash, the one thing I need to bring an end to all of this. It was going to be how I both redeemed and blackmailed him.

Only now do I understand that I never meant to force my father into a public accounting of his crimes. I wanted to win his gambit, corner him, and force him into permanent retirement. He's no longer the CEO of Thorne & Company, and he must no longer be the Leopard. Let him live with what he's done, knowing his daughter was the one who stopped him.

I stare at the tableau. It resembles an Edward Hopper painting, dread and apprehension in every nuance. A portrait of a disaster about to happen. A tragedy about to unfold.

The light gives me the idea. I dash around to the side of the pool terrace, and with one yank on the breaker and using all of my strength, cut the power, submerging the house and everyone inside in total darkness. It's all I can think of to do in the moment. But as I hear my heartbeat pounding in my ears, I dread the imminent sound of a gunshot.

Chapter Eleven

Jerome

I'm ready for him. Luke is behind me, brandishing a bust he yanked off one of the plinths as if he intends to bash in the brains of his former CEO and friend with his own antiquity. I might have found it funny, Mr. Cologne determined to commit murder-by-statue, but nothing about this is funny.

Virgil is here. Right outside. As we pulled up to the house, I caught sight of his fleet figure dashing across the roof. He not only anticipated my move, he made it here before us. It's his house, a city he knows like the back of his hand. And he's not playing around.

If I plan to go through you, you won't even know it until it's over, as I did in Venice.

I'm not about to let him catch me off guard this time.

"Where is he——?"

I hiss Luke to silence, returning my gaze to the terrace flagstones outside the patio doors where his shadow drapes. I intentionally had Luke switch on all the living room lights so Virgil couldn't get inside without me seeing it.

During our drive here, Luke flooring the gas pedal without any respect for the speed limit, I questioned him about every way in and out of the house. He assured me that besides the front door, the patio by the pool was the only other entrance.

"You're sure?" I asked.

"Yes. I mean, I've only stayed in this house a few times, but I recall Virgil mentioning a side gate for the staff by the cottage. You still have to cross the terrace to get to the main house."

"The side gate." I blew air out from the side of my mouth. "Of course. That's how Ania hightailed it out of here."

"You think…?" He glanced at me, passing honking cars as he veered to the canyon exit.

"That tuna sandwich was fresh. She must have heard us arriving and took off. No time to hide the sandwich. Or the sketches she'd thrown in the trash."

"So, she saw us. Which means she knows you're in Los Angeles."

"That would be my bet. She might have been at the party, after all."

"No." He took the canyon road as if he were auditioning to be a stunt driver. The man had a death wish when it came to driving. "I looked for her. I would have recognized her. She couldn't possibly have been there."

"Don't be so sure of it. She managed to do this much without us knowing it."

He frowned at my remark, and once we reached the house, followed my instructions. "No heroics," I warned him. "Stay behind me, no matter what. The Leopard wasn't known for using guns during his heists, and he always did his work after-hours, in secret, in the dark. He changed his pattern in Cannes, though. Brought a gun. I wouldn't put it past him to bring one here."

Luke seized a small bust off the plinth.

Now, we're both sweating like hogs as we wait. I set the case where it would be seen even from the road. I want Virgil to know it's here but not that I'm waiting for him. But, of course, he'll suspect it. He's not going to take any chances with me, either.

The glass terrace doors slide open. I brace for his intrusion—finally time to take down the Leopard. I have to keep myself in check, not rush out in my own ill-timed heroics and end up with a bullet in my gut.

I can hear Luke breathing fast behind me as the figure, dressed head-to-toe in black and a ski mask, for crying out loud—the guy must revel in his master-thief theatrics—steps into the living room. I remind myself to stay cool. I have to catch Virgil in the act, case in hand.

He goes still as if he can sense us hiding around the corner in the hallway. My finger twitches on the trigger. Then he sidles to the case, reaching for it, taking it up and turning—

"Hands up, pal." I step forward with my gun aimed at him.

He freezes.

"That's right. Nice and slow. Case down and step away. Get on the floor, hands behind you. Do it now. I have no problem shooting you in the leg and doing it for you."

He looks as if he's actually considering it, his head cocking. And at that very moment, the lights go out, plunging the entire house into darkness.

I shout. Virgil turns into a smear, darting out the open patio doors, and Luke lunges to fling the hoisted bust straight across the room, smashing the glass patio doors.

It's too late. Virgil's already outside. I bolt after him, hit the coffee table and trip, a sharp pain lancing my knee. Stumbling, I lose my balance but stagger up and race outside, Luke right behind me. The black-clad figure flees across the terrace to the caretakers' cottage.

"Try to cut him off," I bellow at Luke and scramble down the stone steps, ripping my tux and my arm on something sharp at the top of the fence. He's already scaling it. I haul myself up and over—I really have to quit smoking; I'm already winded like I ran a marathon—and throw my entire body at the figure, tackling it to the ground.

"You goddamn sonofabitch," I hiss, leveling my fist to punch him senseless. "Give me that fucking case—"

Except he isn't carrying the case. And I find myself staring in disbelief into Ania's infuriated ice-blue eyes. She doesn't give me time to say anything.

"He's getting away!" she cries, and Luke pulls up seconds later in the car.

Good thing Mr. Cologne is at the wheel because I'm out of breath, bruised, and lacerated, and, to be honest, in a bit of shock. Ania is here, sleek as a cat in black, her hair in a tight bun at her nape, her face scrubbed clean. She looks breathtaking to me, if too thin, and she's urging Luke after a car ahead with a ferocity that has me in the backseat holding on for dear life. The taillights of Virgil's car ahead bounce and scatter as he takes the road at a speed that defies comprehension, and when Ania says, "Faster," Luke hits the gas pedal, and we zoom around a corner at such velocity, I feel the tires lift off the asphalt and hear the screeching skid.

"NO!" Ania screams. But the car ahead has sped up even more to reach the exit to the freeway overpass, and the Cadillac isn't made for high-intensity chases. It's a luxury convertible designed for men like Luke to show off. And as skilled a driver as he is, he loses control as we take the next steep curve.

I duck in the backseat as a loud, hissing pop sounds, followed by our careen off the road and into an embankment with a grinding, teeth-slamming halt.

"No, no! Goddamnit!" Ania curses and flings open the car door to get out, staring toward the escaping car, already a dot as it hits the freeway.

Luke bangs the steering wheel repeatedly with his fist while I clamber out and bend over, feeling like I might vomit out the little I ate at the party.

"How many times can he do this?" Ania swerves to me in a rage as if I'm to blame.

"You've gotta be kidding." I stare right back at her. I'm not sure if I want to kiss her or shout. "What the hell were you doing? Are you nuts? I could have shot you! I thought you were him!"

She goes immobile, taking in my appearance, my pants ripped at the knees and my jacket lost somewhere between the caretakers' cottage and my clamber over the fence, my arm bleeding from whatever I cut it on, a piece of the fence or shattered glass in the living room.

"You shouldn't have interfered," she finally says in a voice that could slice diamonds. "I had him right where I wanted him."

"Oh, you did, did you? Didn't look like it to me."

"I did. Until *you* showed up. You were going to *shoot* him."

I meet her stare. It opens an abyss inside me. "Did you...cut the power to the house?"

She doesn't answer. Luke slides out of the car.

"Why?" I ask her. "Are you helping him now? Have you decided to join the family business in more ways than one?"

Ania throws out her hand as if to hit me. Luke detains her with a droll, "Darling, as delighted as we are to see you alive, I do think you owe us an explanation."

She glares. "I was trying to catch him in the act, to see where he's stashing the loot."

"What loot?" I ask her. "He just got away with it."

She gives one of her exasperated looks. "He must have hidden the rest of it somewhere. He never sold any of it. Never dismantled the pieces or moved any of the gemstones, right?"

"Not that I know of, no."

"Then it stands to reason," she goes on, as if any of this is reasonable, "he's been keeping it somewhere. Like…like trophies from his kills. Up in his tree, as a leopard would do."

"His tree…" I'm having trouble absorbing her words. An entire year without seeing or hearing from her. Months spent in London, calling her office and Luke repeatedly, trying to track down leads. Months of anger and sorrow and, yes, anguish. My heart broken, though men aren't supposed to have their hearts broken. And now she's right here next to me, declaring her intent as if it should make perfect sense. I don't have the strength to tell her just how pissed off I am.

"He must have kept all of it to gloat over. He took one-of-a-kind pieces, all rare and very valuable—some of it priceless. Our own Lemon Twist. He didn't just throw it all away." She's talking as if she's spent the past year thinking of nothing else. As if her every waking minute has been devoted to dismantling her father's methodology. And as it strikes me that it's probably because she *ha*s been doing nothing else but scheming to catch him red-handed, she adds, "I searched everywhere for a hidden place in the house. He once told me that everything in LA is an illusion, and everyone who lives here has an angle. And he had his favorite saying: '*We are all in the gutter, but some of us are looking at the stars,*' inscribed in the house. It has to be a sign. He never did anything without it carrying a double meaning."

"And so, you thought he stashed all of it…?" I glance at Luke in sudden concern.

"I'm *not* crazy." Ania notices the quick look that passes between us. "None of it was in the vault in our New York penthouse. And he'd never leave it in the houses we own in Europe. Not in the palazzo in Venice, and definitely not my apartment in Paris. He stole for a very specific reason. It wasn't for the money. Or the fame. He did it to keep our company on top."

"You've obviously given this a great deal of thought," Luke says.

"Of course, I have. I'm responsible! I couldn't stop him in Venice and—" She cuts herself off, averting her gaze. "It's my responsibility to stop him. He's my father."

I'm starting to understand. She didn't leave me in Venice. She left our circumstances. She saw what could happen, what Virgil was capable of if I stayed involved. He'd set me up to take the fall over the Lemon Twist, and I nearly ended up behind bars. It frightened her enough to cut me loose.

She didn't leave me. If I can only bring myself to believe it.

"None of the jewelry ever showed up on Interpol reports as having been confiscated as contraband," she says. "I hired someone reliable to check the records. If he didn't sell any of it, what did he do with it? This is our only residence where no one would think to search for it."

"Maybe if you'd let me shoot him, we could have asked," I say, bringing her eyes flaring back to me. "He just made off with more of your jewels, the ones you made for Eva Elain. Good thing the second suite was delayed, huh, or Eva would be going to the Oscars in a very bad mood."

"I thought…" Ania falters. "I didn't want you to kill him."

Luke says quietly, "Ania, what else did you think, besides finding his elusive stash?"

"To take away everything he stole! Like he took everything from me." Her voice fractures. "To get my life back."

Luke looks as though he might embrace her. But he doesn't; he knows her too well for that. Instead, he turns to the wrecked car and says, "Darling, why didn't you just ask? I remember when your father had the house built after your mother died. He worked very closely with the architect he hired. The plans are in our archives in New York. All you had to do was ask, and I'd have sent them to you. If he put a hidden place in the house, he must have included it in the plans so it could be built, one would assume."

Ania stares at him. And to my incredulity, and also my relief, a burst of laughter escapes her. She's never been much for laughing, but since I met her, not much has been conducive to it. We fell into each other's lives after the Leopard stole her entire collection in Cannes. And while she's shown me her passionate side, the vibrant woman under her icy façade whom I fell in love with, she's always been on the razor's edge—and it's only gotten worse. Venice, I realize, was a calamity for her. A turning point that upended her existence as much as it did mine.

"All this time." She runs a trembling hand over her mouth. "Trying to protect you, Luke, from the truth, and Jerome from my father, only to end up here. Like in Paris. The three of us by a crashed car while he gets away."

"It's messed up," I rasp, evaporating her mirth. "And this time, there's no hunting him down again. He's been warned. He'll go to ground."

"No." She clenches her fingers. "We can still find him. Find his stash."

"I could fly to New York to fetch those plans," Luke offers. "You have your jet here, yes?" He looks at Ania. "I can go and get them, see if they'll show us anything."

"Yes." She swallows. "Why not? Thank you."

"But first, the car." Luke turns to me. "I'm hopeless when it comes to repairing these contraptions, but I believe it's just a crushed fender and this flat front tire."

"Yeah." I limp to the trunk. "Should be a spare back here."

It's not easy to jack up the car in the embankment, but we only ran off the road when the tire blew, so it's not like we're trapped in a ditch. After I replace it, we manage to slowly and bumpily drive back to the house to retrieve the station wagon and take Luke to the airport. We have to stop at his hotel for him to pack an overnight bag, but for a guy who seems to travel for a weekend trip with ten suitcases, he's surprisingly efficient. The delay allows enough time for Ania to phone the airport, get the jet fueled, and the flight plans filed.

We leave Luke with his promise to return in forty-eight hours with the blueprints.

Then Ania and I return to the house in utter silence, alone at last but too exhausted and uncertain about what to say now that we're suddenly together again. Or not together.

I'm not sure which it is.

The living room is in shambles, the patio doors smashed and glass littering the carpet. Ania takes a broom and dustbin from a closet and starts to sweep it up. I pour myself a scotch at the bar, down it in one gulp, then join her, retrieving the bust that Luke threw, which is remarkably intact, or maybe chipped. But it was pretty chipped already. It's a museum relic, so who knows?

"You should see to that arm," she says as I bend over the pile of glass she's piled up. "Take a hot shower and clean it. There's some gauze and disinfectant in the bathroom and extra clothing in the master bedroom closet. Sweaters. Some pants. It's my father's, but your tuxedo is ruined and..."

"Right. Sure."

In the master suite, I strip and turn on the shower. The hot water strikes my body and brings the nascent aches and bruises to the surface. My knee is swollen but not badly. I wash my arm and see that the wound is jagged but doesn't require stitches—a shallow cut. Some disinfectant, a bandage, and I'll live. I'm going to hurt all over tomorrow, but that's what I get for playing the hero.

After I disinfect and bind my arm, I pad out with a towel around my waist to check the closet. I don't want to touch much less wear any of these expensive items, but I can't walk around naked. Until I can get back to my apartment tomorrow, I'll have to deal with it. It's just clothes. Though we haven't said a word about it, it seems we're staying here for tonight.

Then I hear Ania say softly from behind me, "Let me. There are things there he never wore. Christmas gifts we gave him but weren't up to his exacting taste."

"Really?" I say as she parts the hangers.

She selects a light beige knit pullover and loose black drawstring pants, like pajama bottoms. "I gave him these. I found them in this tiny, out-of-the-way shop in Paris owned by an Algerian tailor. He was a marvel. He made all these simple clothes himself, but my father wasn't impressed. They should fit you. He's tall, like you—"

Her voice chokes in her throat. She extends the clothes, and despite the darkness of the bedroom, lit only by the bathroom light, I can see moisture glistening in her eyes.

"I really messed up, didn't I?" she whispers.

"You tried," I hear myself reply. "Can't regret it now." I take the clothes from her, awkward because one of my hands still holds the towel at my waist. As I turn to the bathroom to get dressed, she says, "I'm sorry."

I go still.

"I...I shouldn't have done it."

"Done what?" Now, *my* voice is tightening up.

"All of it. The heist in Venice. Leaving you like I did. This. I thought..." A ragged exhale. "I guess I didn't think. I wanted to catch him so badly I didn't think it all through. I thought I had."

"You did okay." I glance over my shoulder and see her perched on the edge of the bed. "It was a good plan. Those leopard heads on the jewelry were a particularly nice touch. Classy."

She gazes at me, standing with the clothes in one hand and the towel gripped in my other. "I've seen it before, you know. I've seen you naked."

"Uh…" It's just two steps to her, and it abruptly feels like a chasm. "What are you saying?"

"I want you, Jerome." Her voice is barely a whisper. "I never stopped wanting you. I never stopped…thinking of you. But I couldn't—I couldn't let him hurt you again." She lowers her eyes. Stands. "Forget it. I must be crazy. You must hate me."

I drop the clothes. I almost drop the towel, too. "I don't."

She pauses.

"I don't hate you, Ania. I think you're batshit crazy for doing all of this, but…I kind of like this side of you. Out of control. It's sexy, in a very weird and messed-up way."

And then I move to her, cup her chin, and lift her face to look into those beautiful eyes, brimming with unshed tears like tiny diamonds formed from the dust in her veins. That small, perfect face that now appears so very young without makeup, stripped of her status. Just a woman. A gorgeous one who's too thin and built like a ballerina. Has she been surviving on tuna fish sandwiches and arugula for the entire year?

Her mouth tastes dry from waning adrenaline and fear, but her lips are so soft. Hesitant at first, so it takes me a moment before I crush her against me, feeling every muscle and taut bone, and my body responds to her despite my bruises and cuts. I'm desperate for her. I feel her hands slide past my stomach. The towel falls, and I think that if she touches me there, I'll explode. When her arms come up around my neck, it's like nothing I've ever felt. For a second, I almost start to cry.

She feels like home.

I don't think of anything. I just want to get lost in her. I want to feel all of her. I lift her and set her on the bed, slide off her black clothes, the lacy underwear—black, too—and reveal her pale, exquisite length. She has a mottled bruise on her thigh, likely from climbing the fence, when I tackled her to the ground, or the crash. I kiss it, and her incised ribs expand as her breath quickens. I'm drowning just doing this. She's everything I've ever wanted, the girl of my dreams, way out of my league. And I don't care. And then I feel her urging me on top of her, her mouth ravenous at my throat and chest. Sense her urgency as she trails downwards. She's taking control, and I let her do it. She takes me, and she uses me, and I buck into her like I'm diving into an endless warm ocean. There's no languid foreplay, no apologies or ardent whispers; she mounts me in ferocious silence, her head thrown back, her hair unraveling to her shoulders in a glistening fall. Darker blond now, not highlighted by regular visits to an expensive beauty salon.

My leopard.

When I moan at the growing intensity of our joining, the pleasure cresting hotly inside me, she stops, leans over me to put her mouth on mine, and breathes, "Let go, Jerome."

And I do.

Afterwards, I can't move. I should see to her, but she's nestled at my side, her hand on my chest, and the sensation of her skin against mine immobilizes me like a sedative.

"I'm so tired…"

"Me, too." She kisses my cheek. "Let's go to sleep."

When I wake the next morning, sunlight drifts dimly through the drawn drapes, and I hurt all over, but I also feel refreshed somehow. I slept like a log.

Slipping into the crumpled clothes I left on the floor, the pullover too loose but the pants easily adjusted by the drawstring, I walk barefoot into the living room, smelling coffee brewing, and then think I should have put my shoes on, there might still be glass on the carpet—

There isn't. Though the patio doors are shells, she's cleaned everything up. It looks the same as it did: immaculate, a movie set waiting for the actors to arrive.

She's outside at the railing of the pool wall, looking upon the city. She's wearing her black outfit, and she turns her head at my approach.

She's much too pale and way too beautiful in the daylight.

"I brought up some coffee from the cottage," she says as I think about my cigarettes, lost in my tux jacket pocket wherever I shed it. Then she adds, "I found your jacket by the fence, too, in case you want to smoke. You always had a cigarette with your morning coffee."

"I don't want to smoke," I reply, thinking that I really don't. "I want to take a swim in that big-ass pool of yours."

"Do it. The water might be cold from the night, but it's clean. We have a pool boy who comes by when the Millers are away."

"That was your idea, too?"

She nods. "I didn't want any witnesses here while I searched the house."

"Smart." I step beside her.

After a long moment, she says, "What are we going to do?"

"Dunno." I shrug. "Wait for Luke, I suppose. In the meantime, I'm starving."

"We're fresh out of everything except for a single can of tuna fish."

"Ugh." I feign a shudder. I want to take her hand, but all of a sudden, the chasm is back. "Let's have some coffee and hit a diner in town. Scrambled eggs and greasy bacon. Then, I don't know, go to my apartment so I can change into something less Virgil and do some sightseeing. I've always wanted to see the handprints at Grauman's Chinese."

"You do?" she says skeptically. "I thought all of this…"

"Yeah, it's fake and pretentious as hell, but I still like the movies."

"And Lauren Segal," she says darkly, out of nowhere. "She likes you, too."

"No." I meet her eyes. She flinches. "She offered me the job because I was drinking and working crap freelance in London. She's a friend. Nothing else happened between us."

She nods, turning toward the house.

"So?" I ask. "Eggs and bacon, then tour LA like tourists from North Dakota? And no talking about any of this, just for today?"

She lets out a faint laugh. "I think I'd like that."

Chapter Twelve

Ania

If I weren't my father's daughter, and he wasn't the Leopard, and Jerome still had his job at Lambert, today is what our life would be like. Maybe not in California, probably in New York or London or maybe Paris, but we're in the land of make-believe today, and that's been the theme of our time together. We are making believe that our lives are normal and that we're living them hand in hand, as tourists from North Dakota, here to see Tinseltown.

We start, as Jerome requested, at a diner we find on Melrose. He has a greasy fry-up, and since I'm pretending that I'm not me, I order pancakes and cover them in butter and boysenberry syrup.

We're not engaging in *figure-important-things-out-now*. We are in limbo, waiting for Luke to return so we can abandon the old script for a while. While we eat, we make a list of places we each want to see, writing them down on a napkin. Five places.

After we've each cleaned our plates and finished our mugs of coffee, we get back into the car. First stop: Grauman's Chinese.

"I can't remember the last time I played tourist," I say as we park and walk toward the famous sidewalk. Jerome surprises me by doing impressions of some of the famous names we come across. It's a side to him that I've never seen. He's lighter, easier, and seems relieved of a burden I didn't realize he had been carrying—but, of course, I should have.

At Roy Rogers' square, which has Trigger's hoofprints embedded in the cement, as well, Jerome gives a long whinny. At John Barrymore's, he launches into a *Hamlet* soliloquy. He sings at Eddie Cantor's imprint, crooning the first few lines of *How Ya Gonna Keep 'em Down on the Farm.* When he finds the Marx Brothers' section, he puts an imaginary cigar to his mouth and impersonates Groucho by moving his eyebrows up and down hilariously and quoting, "A woman is only a woman, but a good cigar is a smoke."

I haven't laughed this hard in—I can't remember how long it's been, and it loosens something like a knot inside me. The day has just started, and I already don't want it to end.

"What's the matter?" Jerome asks.

"Why do you think something's wrong?"

"One minute, you were laughing. And now, your eyes are all sad."

I'm not sure I can answer him. There is too much to say, and this isn't the place to say it.

"I think we should have different names today. No way would we be Jerome and Ania if we're from Oak Avenue in Grand Forks, North Dakota," I say.

"Grand Forks? Is there such a place?"

"There is."

"How do you know that?"

"We had a housekeeper who had a cousin who moved there."

"Okay, Grand Forks it is. What would your name be?"

"No, you name me, and I'll name you."

Jerome nods. Searching for inspiration, he looks up and down the block, reading the names above the signatures.

"Betty," he says finally. "You're Betty."

"And you"—I use the same method of inspiration—"are Tyrone."

"That's not really more all-American than my name, you know. Why did you pick it?"

"Because I had a wicked crush on Tyrone Power." I point to the cement square.

"And you have a wicked crush on me?" He smiles, then pulls me to him and kisses me. Right there on the sidewalk, with stars' handprints all around us. Kissing me in public isn't something he's ever done before.

It starts sweet but heats up quickly. For a moment, I'm lost in his touch and his scent and how his lips seem to push the world away.

He breaks our embrace before I do.

"There's no such thing as a little smooch with you, you know that? Let's hit the next place on our list."

The La Brea Tar Pits is his suggestion. I hadn't even heard of it, but on the way there, he explains. "Bones were first found in the pit in 1901 and recognized as fossils of extinct animals by a Los Angeles geologist. Students started doing excavations there in 1905 and have never stopped."

"How do you know so much about it?"

"I wanted to be an archeologist when I was a kid. I read everything I could get my hands on. I was thinking of going back to college to study archeology, but the war started, and…"

Before I respond, he pulls up and parks.

I didn't know what to expect, but it's not the life-sized mastodon reproductions wading in a small lake in the middle of Los Angeles. We explore the pit and wonder at the sixty-five-million-year-old bones on display in the museum.

Next up is a drive to Santa Monica. The ocean is my choice of touristy things to do. The first sight of that green-blue expanse fills me up. Getting out of the car, I take a deep breath and close my eyes, soaking in the murmur of the waves and the warmth of the sun on my face.

I don't hear Jerome coming up beside me until he's kissing me again.

This kiss ends too fast, as well, but not for the same reason.

"Take off your shoes and come with me," he says.

Then he grabs my hand, and we saunter down to the beach, where we sit and watch the Pacific. It feels so good just to sit there, no plans or worries. We have this day-long reprieve, and I'm determined to enjoy it.

After a while, we stroll down to the water, walking past teenage girls sunning themselves and boys playing volleyball. At the shore's edge, we roll up our pants and wade into the surf.

After a half-hour or so of getting our toes frozen by the surprisingly cold water, we head back up to a hotdog stand and get chili dogs and Cokes, plus a shared order of fries.

"This is some vacation, Betty," Jerome says as he offers me a ketchup-smeared fry.

"I just wish it didn't have to end so soon."

"Maybe it doesn't have to," he says, whispering this time.

I look into his eyes. He's not playing our tourist game now. He means it.

"Maybe it doesn't," I manage to say. "Once this is all resolved, and we've found the loot—"

He puts his finger against my lips. "We're on vacation. No shoptalk, okay?" He sounds jocular, but I saw his eyes darken when I started to mention the Leopard. It bothers him, my father's shadow between us.

I nod and push up on my toes to kiss him. Not a long one, but a thank-you kiss for giving me this time out of my head.

Walking toward the car, we pass a little gift shop, and Jerome pulls me inside.

"I can shop in New York," I say. Not that I've done any of that in the past year.

"But we're not in New York. Your birthday is coming up soon. I want to buy you a present."

I'm surprised he even knows my birthday is in three weeks. It strikes me that in all the time we were together, we never did those ordinary couple things like sharing our birthdays, favorite songs, and books. We were always too driven by our hunt.

"Okay. But, Tyrone, things are expensive here in Los Angeles."

"You deserve it. Besides, my work's been good lately. Got my studio pay."

The shop is a combination antique store and tourist trap. We bypass the items printed with logos of the Hollywood sign and Santa Monica Pier and head for the back where there are racks of vintage clothes and shelves of 1930s hats. Beautiful, old things that I linger over.

"Can I help you?" the young shopkeeper asks.

"We're just looking, but you have such lovely things."

"My father works in Hollywood as a voice coach. The actors give him things to sell," she says. "Sometimes, a studio sells off its props, too."

Jerome is looking into a case filled with glittering objects.

"Can I see that?" he asks.

I walk over and see him pointing to a silver-link bracelet. He gently pushes me away.

"Go try on hats," he says.

I smile and turn away.

A few moments later, he finds me modeling a ridiculously huge straw beach hat.

"You want that? It's very becoming. For Betty."

"I don't think I have anywhere to wear it."

Once we're outside, I expect Jerome to give me whatever he bought, but he doesn't.

Next stop is Schwab's Drug Store for sodas at the famous counter. I have a lime Ricky, and he has a root beer. We put Paramount Studios down on the list, but it's a movie studio, and he's seen one of those. Having spent longer than we expected at the beach, we decide instead to go to the Farmer's Market and buy some food for dinner.

I know they have things already prepared, but Jerome says he wants to make me dinner himself, so we walk through the stands with him picking up items and putting them in a cart. Not being much of a cook myself, I can't guess at what he's making by the purchases, and when I ask, he says it's his specialty, and I'll have to wait.

The day is like a long act of foreplay. Sights and sounds, embraces and tantalizing tastes.

Back at the main house, where I'm not hiding out from anyone anymore, I take a swim, and Jerome busies himself in the kitchen.

I'm still doing laps as the sun begins to set over the hills. He comes out with my terrycloth robe and two glasses of wine. I strip off my bathing suit, and he wraps me in the robe. "I need to take a swim myself," he remarks, but he doesn't. We sit on the patio, sipping the crisp, cold white and watching the fiery colors in the sky darken. We don't speak.

"I'm happy here, Betty," he says at length.

"Me, too, Tyrone."

He smiles and pulls out the silver bracelet from his pocket. The sun glints off the metal, and I recognize the links from my quick glimpse in the store on the boardwalk.

"Give me your wrist," he says.

I hold it out, and he clicks the bracelet around it—a delicate chain with a little Eiffel Tower charm dangling from it.

"We were strangers until Paris," he says. "Sounds like a movie, doesn't it? Paris was where everything changed between us. We're as possible as this impossible tower. I don't want you to forget it, okay?"

Tears sting my eyes, and I blink them away. He's always been more romantic than me, and it's the sweetest present anyone has ever given me. I've never been much for wearing jewelry, as odd as it seems. Working with precious stones and metals is my passion, but wearing what I create would be like a painter wearing one of her canvases. I make art for others, not myself.

This bracelet is different. It's not a piece of jewelry as much as it is a promise, and I touch it gingerly with my forefinger.

Jerome lifts my chin and looks into my eyes. "Getting sentimental in your old age, Betty?"

I lean forward and kiss him.

He's on the chaise lounge, and a moment later, I'm on it with him. I open my robe, and his hands are on my skin. I unbutton his shirt, unbuckle his belt, and pull down his slacks.

As the sun lowers in the sky, I lower myself onto him and gasp as he slides inside of me. There's no space between us, no words that need to be said. Time suspends as our bodies answer a primal rhythm.

Unlike last night, when I was so overcome by my need for him that I took charge, I allow him to guide us. He takes his time, and it feels like coming home after an achingly long absence. We move slowly, in unison, in *wonder* at how it feels to be together this way, with a slightly cool breeze drifting over us as we make love and night falls over the city of angels.

I stay on top of him as he strokes my hair. I sense that as much as he gave of himself just now, he's still holding something back. It was in his eyes on the boardwalk, a somber distancing when I mentioned the loot, and it's here now in the way his hand moves slowly over my hair. It saddens me because I know his hesitancy isn't because he's unsure of his feelings. It's my obsession that's built this unbreachable wall between us. He doesn't trust that I won't hurt or leave him again. I can't blame him for it, but I also can't say the words he needs to hear. I already know, in the pit of my stomach, that if the architectural plans don't turn up my father's stash, I won't be able to stay. I'll have to resume my hunt.

Until the Leopard is captured, I can never rest or have a moment's peace again.

And I think Jerome knows it, too.

Over an amazing dinner of what turns out to be spaghetti in a delicious homemade tomato sauce with a robust Chianti wine and fresh garlic bread, we talk about the day, about the sights, and steer the conversation from the very thing that's keeping us together.

We manage to avoid the shoals, but all the unvoiced uncertainties are at the table with us.

We open another bottle of wine and return to the patio, both of us having a little too much to drink in our attempt to stave off the end of this wonderful day. But when it does end, we fall into bed and sleep soundly, wrapped tightly around each other.

Luke phones us at the house upon arriving the following afternoon with the plans. He made the roundtrip to New York in forty-eight hours, and he looks it when he arrives in a taxi, shadows under his eyes, and his clothing rumpled—a first for him. After he takes a shower and changes, I make him a sandwich, and we spread the plans out on the dining room table to pore over.

"Here." Jerome points at what appears to be an area designed to be built under the pool. "This looks like it could be it."

"It's not," I say reluctantly. "I know this house. I've searched every inch of it, and there's no entry into any area under the pool. Maybe they planned for it, but it was never actually built."

Jerome goes silent, contemplating the plans. Then he says, "I used to hunt down fugitive Nazis. You wouldn't believe the cubbyholes they could crawl into. If this area was put into the plans and was, in fact, built, maybe the way inside was deliberately kept secret."

"So, how do we find it?" asks Luke, pouring himself a glass of wine. "I'm dead on my feet. Flying to and from New York without so much as an overnight stay is deadly on one's constitution. I highly do *not* recommend it. I tried to sleep on the plane, but there was too much turbulence, so if we're going to do something, let's start before I fall onto this sofa and pass out."

"We should check every piece of flooring and every wall in the house from top to bottom," Jerome says, widening Luke's tired eyes. "Look for a false wall or an opening or lever."

"Every piece and every inch…?" echoes Luke in dismay.

"If they built something under the pool, there has to be a way to get inside it," Jerome insists.

I touch the little Eiffel Tower on my bracelet and hope he's right.

Chapter Thirteen

Jerome

It's not a big house. I mean, it's bigger than anything I've lived in, but not a mansion. Only three bedrooms: the master suite and two guest rooms—so, modest for a rich person. A private getaway where Virgil didn't expect to have many visitors or do much in the way of entertaining. His home in the hills over the city he ended up hating. Three bathrooms and a powder room off the living area. Add in the living room, the dining area, the kitchen, and his study, and you've pretty much covered it. Of course, there's also the terrace and grounds, so still plenty for us to search.

Luke looks as if I asked him to crawl through the catacombs of Egypt. I divide us, Ania with Luke, and me alone because I can work faster that way. Still, it takes hours, tapping on walls and flooring, opening every closet and cabinet, pulling back rugs—not many of those—and checking behind every painting and bookshelf. The statue plinths are bolted to the floor, but I still try to shift them to see if anything is hidden under them. The house's clean austerity helps, no extraneous clutter, but night has fallen outside by the time we regroup, and Ania rakes her fingers impatiently through her hair.

"Nothing." Her voice is pinched. "Not a damn thing."

"Well." I suddenly crave a cigarette when I haven't smoked all day and didn't miss it. "Let's think. What did we miss?"

"We didn't." She leans against the sofa as Luke collapses on it. "I thought…I must have been wrong. He didn't hide any of it here."

I don't like the severity in her tone. She's been almost like herself and more relaxed than I've ever seen her lately. Without her work—when we were traveling together, she was either waiting for important papers to arrive, mailing important documents to her office, scheduling meetings on the phone, or preparing for a call—and with our agreed-upon moratorium on anything Leopard-related, she became who I believe she's supposed to be. She toured the city with me. Ate hotdogs at a beach stand for crissakes—a woman who nibbles on salads and pâté.

And she waded in the surf. I can still hear her squeal when the ocean seeped over her bare toes. "*It's freezing! I thought you could swim in California,*" and it made me realize that as many times as she's been here, she never actually felt the ocean. She never did any of the things we do when we visit other places. Her life of high privilege kept her in a cage, every hour scheduled in advance: from her private plane to the hired car to the five-star hotel or family residence. Luxury stores and gourmet meals. No wandering off to get lost. No exploration for the delight of discovery.

It hurt my soul to think that she's lived all her life in some kind of luxurious prison.

"We must have missed something." My eyes lift to the saying inscribed in steel letters above the window: *"We are all in the gutter, but some of us are looking at the stars."*

"The gutter," I say aloud.

"What?" Ania frowns. From the sofa, Luke adds wearily, "I feel like I've been dragged through one. This jet lag is appalling. Please tell me he's not thinking of actually obliging us to search the gutters outside."

"No." I look at Ania. "The plans indicate an area was to be built under the pool. How's it maintained? There must be—I don't know, a pump house or something. Something to shelter the guts. The filtration system and whatnot."

Her frown brings her eyebrows together. "There's a pump house outside, past the cottage, right by the cliff. But it's—"

I bolt out the door. She follows and calls to me to wait while she turns on those little path lamps, but I'm already bounding through the darkness. It's not easy to find in the night, a concrete hut-like structure hidden in overgrowth, but the well-tended path leads me right to it.

"Is it locked?" I ask as she comes up behind me.

"Why would it be?" She pushes on the steel door, and it grinds open, releasing a musty smell of dampness. A horde of disturbed mosquitoes flitter out, and she shudders.

"Jerome, there can't possibly be an entrance in there."

"Get me a flashlight," I tell her, peering into the gloom and hearing the muted hum of machinery, the filtration system at work.

"Really?"

I nod. "Really."

She goes to the cottage and returns with one. I switch it on and direct the beam inside. Less than an inch of water on the floor and the hunched shapes of coiled pipes.

Ania hovers at the door as I move in, easing around the pump to shine the light across the block walls. It's a bunker-like construction on the steep decline of the hillside where the house is perched. All of a sudden, I'm certain it has to be here. Memories of bombed-out buildings, little more than skeletons, assault me. Creeping to the designated spot with my team, knowing the man we hunted was inside, hidden behind a crumbled wall or in a hole dug under rubble. I captured several low-level German bureaucrats that way, most of them going to ground after Berlin fell, all of them with blood on their hands from stamping documents that sent thousands to die in the camps.

Sidling around the pump, I start rapping on the block walls, listening closely for hollowness. It's solid all the way around, but as I go lower, getting on my knees in the bilge water, checking each section, I finally detect it—a loose block at the bottom of the back wall.

Pulling it out, I reveal the lever it concealed.

"Come here," I say. Still at the doorway, Ania replies, "I'm wearing Chanel flats. You can't possibly expect me to—"

"Ania. Forget your shoes. It's here."

She plunges into the room, sloshing across the water. She goes immobile, staring at where I'm pointing the flashlight.

"Want to do the honors?" I ask.

"I...I can't," she whispers in disbelief.

I pull on the lever. A section of the back wall creaks open.

Ania breathes. "An illusion, like a movie backdrop. Just as my father told me. Everything in LA is fake."

"His tree." I meet her eyes but can't tell if it's relief or fear I see in them. "You were right."

I step aside as she tentatively moves into the Leopard's lair.

Chapter Fourteen

Ania

Entering my father's hiding place is like stepping into a secret jewelry box. I think of the ruby-colored leather one I had growing up with the ballerina on top that danced when I wound her up. The song was *La Vie en Rose* and, bizarrely, I can hear it in my head now as I stare in awe at the display before me. My ballerina isn't here, but the interior of this jewelry box is so similar to the one I had long ago. The overhead light that Jerome switches on illuminates the priceless treasures on suede-lined shelves along the length of the vault, though how my father managed to keep the damp from seeping in eludes me. Did he have this room insulated?

The space is small, just big enough for a man of my father's size to come down here to gloat over his hoard. A bit crowded for two people. The vault is probably no more than five feet wide and five feet deep, and from how the top of Jerome's head almost skims the ceiling, no more than seven feet high. An industrial-type carpet covers the floor. The walls are steel beyond the shelving, and there's an ordinary wooden stool pushed up against one end of the vault. It's chilly down here, the way it always is underground, and it makes me shiver. *It might not be the temperature*, I think as I stare at the bounty displayed on the shelves.

I shouldn't be surprised to see all these pieces of missing jewelry. I believed with all my heart that my father had hidden them somewhere and that, eventually, I would find them. And yet, I'm still in a state of shock. Not sure if it's the reality of the discovery or the mesmerizing beauty of the stones that renders me speechless. I hadn't even realized quite how many pieces he had taken over the years.

Here are all the items stolen from his rivals. There's my Cannes collection, every last piece of it. Over there are famed, one-of-a-kind jewelry items he lifted from wealthy women. When I spot the Lemon Twist, I reach out to touch the canary-diamond center stone. It's like reuniting with an old friend whom I'd thought I would never see again.

"Look what's here," says Jerome.

I go to his side and look down at a tray of loose diamonds, unable to place them for a second until I realize with a jolt in my stomach that they must be the stones that cost the jewel cutter's assistant her life in London.

"My God," I whisper, horrified.

The cold, glittering stones are frightening in their indifference.

I spin around, taking in all the jewelry, not focusing on any piece but on the insanity of it as a whole. Millions of dollars' worth. His loot from every heist, stashed here underground—the sum of my father's crimes. I feel the weight of what he has done in a way that's entirely new to me, and I don't realize I've slid down to the floor until I feel cold steel against my back through the fabric of my blouse.

I'm shaking now—frightened and confused.

Jerome sits beside me and puts his arm around me. I must be holding myself too stiffly because as he takes hold of me, I feel a knot in my chest dissolve, and tears fill my eyes.

"Why?" I ask him. "Why did he do it? Why take all of it only to leave it here, seen by no one but him? What was the reason for any of it?"

With his thumb, Jerome wipes away my tears with that gentility he shows now when he touches me as if I'm made of glass.

It's not a question I expect him to answer. After all, I explained it myself after the car went off the road and had already explained it to Jerome in Venice. But now, being here, having discovered my father's tree, his lair, the overwhelming truth is too much for me. The evidence is undeniable. I can no longer hold out hope that I've been wrong in thinking I never knew my father.

When my mother died, *Tante* Marie told me that the hardest thing to give up in the world is hope. She said it keeps us from the depths of despair. Allows us to keep breathing, to envision a better time. Gives us the chance to dream. But when hope goes, you're left with emptiness. And that's how I feel now.

Jerome brushes my hair from my face and says in a quiet voice, "You told me yourself why he did it. Virgil never wanted to sell or dismantle the jewelry. He didn't do it because he needed money. He did it to feed his ego, vanity, and reputation by stealing from his competitors and costing them millions in losses. It's how he kept Thorne & Company on top."

"But he lost control of the company anyway. And he lost me."

Something in me hardens as I admit that. I'm done shedding tears over a man who did not live up to who I thought he was. He hasn't been my father or my hero for a long time. I'm ready to let go of any illusions that I can find a reason to justify his actions.

"He didn't intend to lose control of the company," Jerome says. "Or you. That was his mistake." He pauses, seeing my gaze stray to the shelves, drawn as though I'm hypnotized. "What are you going to do now that you've found it?"

"I came looking for it for one reason," I reply at once because I'm sure of this much. "To make reparations. All these stolen items must be returned to their rightful owners."

"A noble goal. You'll be a heroine—albeit a tragic one, given who the thief is."

I swallow and force myself to meet his stare. "I can't do that. I don't want Thorne & Company connected to any of this. I still want…I *need* to protect the company. Not for my father or for myself, but I have employees across the globe. People like Luke, who depend on me to earn their living. If I reveal who did this, we'll never survive it."

"Then, what…?" His question lingers.

"I was hoping you'd do it for me. Jerome, I've thought this out. Figured if we found the loot, you could do it. You'll make headlines: The insurance investigator who finally cracked the Leopard's secret stash. You can't reveal his identity, but you'll get your job back at Lambert or any other security firm you want to work for. You'll be swamped with offers. A hero. It's the least I can do after everything I've put you through."

"I'm an *ex*-insurance investigator," he says, drawing in a troubled breath.

"So?" I didn't realize that I'd been crying through my little speech until I hear my sob break in the back of my throat like a punctuation point.

Jerome is very quiet until he says, "And I can't do it, either."

Chapter Fifteen

Jerome

"Why not?" Her voice tightens, but her tears dry up fast. "You can't think to *penalize* me for it, force me to go public with my father's identity. The company isn't to blame. It didn't steal—"

I give her a look that silences her outburst. Wow, she has the quickest temper of any woman I've ever known, and it's going to take some getting used to. Times past, I'd thought I would have to set off a bomb or stand before her stark-naked to get a reaction out of her.

"I'm not saying that. I'm saying I'll do it because it's the right thing to do, but only if I can do it quietly. Some of this loot is decades old. No one wants front-page headlines, especially me. To return items thought long-lost is enough compensation. I bet a few of the rightful owners may have died by now—the Leopard stole from old ladies as well as young ones—but their children will appreciate the gesture. That jeweler's assistant, nothing will bring her back. But the jeweler will probably really like to get his diamonds back."

"Oh." She nods, standing uncertainly. She knows she went off half-cocked, but at least this is the Ania I know. She was never very good at apologies. Confrontation makes her anxious, and she sometimes forgets to say, "I'm sorry," though she feels it.

"That's it?" she asks at length. "That's all you want?"

I almost laugh. Besides forgetting to apologize, she can be so blind.

"No, that's not all I want." I stand, too. I suddenly want to get out of this vault. It's giving me the creeps. "All I've ever wanted from the start of all this is to be with you, but I guess that's impossible. He got away, and you won't stop until you catch him, will you?"

She averts her eyes. Yeah, I prefer that. I don't think I'm going to like her answer, but I have to give it a try. Like her, I've been giving it a lot of thought.

"Unless you can accept that you've already caught him."

She flinches and looks up at me.

"None of this is his anymore," I go on. "The Leopard no longer exists. Your father escaped, but he's just Virgil Thorne now. A man on the run. You've won, Ania. You proved who's better. I understand if you can't let it go, but I don't like it. He took away the father who taught you what you love to do. The man you trusted. He took away everything you believed in. I guess you have the right to look him in the face and get back whatever you can from him."

Ania goes still. Then she reaches into her pocket, the little Eiffel Tower dangling from her wrist, and removes a pair of crumpled leopard-print gloves. She hands them to me. "He didn't take away everything. I want it to end. I can't give him you, the one thing I love the most."

Well, knock me over with a feather. I stand there with my mouth hanging open like an idiot, those hated gloves, a symbol of the nightmare he put us both through, clasped in my hand.

"You mean it?" I manage to say.

She smiles. Oh, that smile. I could melt at her feet. "I do."

"What about the suite you designed for the studio? I mean, it's a chunk of change and you can't file a claim if you don't report it stolen, which, if you do, will take some explaining."

"Let him have it. His last trophy. I don't care anymore."

I can't move an inch as she steps toward me. "I don't want to lose you," she whispers.

I reach out, seize her and kiss her, right there amid the loot, and it feels like I've finally come home. She's pliant and taut; she's silk and claw. My leopard.

We return to the pool area where Luke is pacing. He turns to us. His face brightens into a smile, fatigued but visibly relieved.

"Well?" he asks as the three of us lean against the railing, taking in the sunset over Los Angeles. A vivid red and orange like flames streaked across the sky. "It's about time you two ironed things out. I was starting to think I might have to sit each of you down and give you a lecture on how rare true love is. And, Ania, my dearest, as much as I adore you, running your company while chasing after a thief has wreaked havoc on my nerves. Your uncle Luke needs a long vacation in a hot climate, preferably with plenty of alcohol and matadors in skintight pants."

Ania's burst of laughter kicks up warmth in my heart. She's laughing, with an effervescence I've never seen in her before. She's laughing as if the weight of the world has fallen from her shoulders. As if she's a child again and believes all her dreams will come true.

I feel the same weight drop from me as she wraps her hand tightly around mine. I give Luke a grin. "Why matadors? I mean, I get that they fight bulls in silly outfits, so they're brave and all that, but of all the men in the world…"

"You really want me to tell you?" he says with a sigh. Ania chuckles.

"No," I say at once but keep grinning at him because Mr. Cologne has proven to be the friend that I never thought I'd have. Way out of my league, maybe, like she is.

But, hey, who cares?

A new friend. The girl of my dreams. How did a slob like me get so damn lucky?

THE END

* * * *

Also from Blue Box Press, C. W. Gortner, and M.J. Rose, discover The Steal and The Bait.

The Steal

By C. W. Gortner and M.J. Rose

They say diamonds are a girl's best friend—until they're stolen.

Ania Throne is devoted to her jewelry company. The daughter of one of the world's most famous jewelers, she arrives in Cannes with a stunning new collection. But a shocking theft by the notorious thief known as the Leopard throws her into upheaval—and plunges her on an unexpected hunt that challenges everything she believes.

Jerome Curtis thinks he's seen it all, especially when it comes to crime. Until he's hired to investigate the loss of Ania Thorne's collection, his every skill put to the test as he chases after a mysterious master-mind responsible for some of the costliest heists in history—and finds himself in a tangled web with a woman he really shouldn't fall in love with.

From the fabled Carlton Hotel to the elegant boulevards of Paris, Ania and Jerome must race against time to catch a thief before the thief catches them. With everything on the line, can they solve the steal or will the steal take more than diamonds from them?

Set in the late 1950s, THE STEAL is a romantic caper by bestselling authors C.W. Gortner and M.J. Rose.

Mademoiselle Chanel
By C.W. Gortner

A stunning novel of iconic fashion designer Coco Chanel—who revolutionized fashion, built an international empire, and become one of the most influential and controversial figures of the twentieth century.

Born into rural poverty, Gabrielle Chanel and her siblings are sent to orphanage after their mother's death. The sisters nurture Gabrielle's exceptional sewing skills, a talent that will propel her into a life far removed from the drudgery of her childhood.

Transforming herself into Coco—a seamstress and sometime torch singer—the petite brunette burns with an incandescent ambition that draws a wealthy gentleman who will become the love of her life. She immerses herself in his world of money and luxury, discovering a freedom that sparks her creativity. But it is only when her lover takes her to Paris that Coco discovers her destiny.

Rejecting the frilly, corseted silhouette of the past, her sleek, minimalist styles reflect the youthful ease and confidence of the 1920s modern woman. As Coco's reputation spreads, her couturier business explodes, taking her into rarefied society circles and bohemian salons. But her fame and fortune cannot save her from heartbreak as the years pass. And when Paris falls to the Nazis, she is forced to make choices that will haunt her.

Mademoiselle Chanel explores the inner world of a woman of staggering ambition whose strength, passion and artistic vision would become her trademark.

The Last Tiara
By M.J. Rose

A provocative and moving story of a young female architect in post-World War II Manhattan who stumbles upon a hidden treasure and begins a journey to discovering her mother's life during the fall of the Romanovs.

Sophia Moon had always been reticent about her life in Russia and when she dies, suspiciously, on a wintry New York evening, Isobelle despairs that her mother's secrets have died with her. But while renovating the apartment they shared, Isobelle discovers something among her mother's effects — a stunning silver tiara, stripped of its jewels.

Isobelle's research into the tiara's provenance draws her closer to her mother's past — including the story of what became of her father back in Russia, a man she has never known. The facts elude her until she meets a young jeweler who wants to help her but is conflicted by his loyalty to the Midas Society, a covert international organization whose mission is to return lost and stolen antiques, jewels, and artwork to their original owners.

Told in alternating points of view, the stories of the two young women unfurl as each struggles to find their way during two separate wars. In 1915, young Sofiya Petrovitch, favorite of the royal household and best friend of Grand Duchess Olga Nikolaevna, tends to wounded soldiers in a makeshift hospital within the grounds of the Winter Palace in St. Petersburg and finds the love of her life. In 1948 New York, Isobelle Moon works to break through the rampant sexism of the age as one of very few women working in a male-dominated profession and discovers far more about love and family than she ever hoped for.

In the two narratives, the secrets of Sofiya's early life are revealed incrementally, even as Isobelle herself works to solve the mystery of the historic Romanov tiara (which is based on an actual Romanov artifact that is, to this day, still missing) and how it is that her mother came to possess it. The two strands play off each other in finely-tuned counterpoint, building to a series of surprising and deeply satisfying revelations.

About C. W. Gortner

C.W. GORTNER holds an MFA in Writing with an emphasis in Renaissance Studies from the New College of California, as well as an AA from the Fashion Institute of Design and Merchandising in San Francisco.

After an eleven year-long career in fashion, C.W. devoted the next twelve years to the public health sector. In 2012, he became a full-time writer following the international success of his novels.

In his extensive travels to research his books, he has danced a galliard at Hampton Court, learned about organic gardening at Chenoceaux, and spent a chilly night in a ruined Spanish castle. His books have garnered widespread acclaim and been translated into twenty-one languages to date. C.W. is also a dedicated advocate for animal rights, in particular companion animal rescue to reduce shelter overcrowding.

Half-Spanish by birth and raised in southern Spain, C.W. lives in Northern California with his husband and two very spoiled rescue cats.

To find out more about his work, visit: http://www.cwgortner.com

About M.J. Rose

New York Times, USAToday, and *Wall St. Journal* bestseller, M.J. Rose grew up in New York City mostly in the labyrinthine galleries of the Metropolitan Museum, the dark tunnels and lush gardens of Central Park and reading her mother's favorite books before she was allowed. She believes mystery and magic are all around us but we are too often too busy to notice... books that exaggerate mystery and magic draw attention to it and remind us to look for it and revel in it.

Rose's work has appeared in many magazines including Oprah Magazine and The Adventurine and she has been featured in the New York Times, Newsweek, WSJ, Time, USA Today and on the Today Show, and NPR radio.

Rose graduated from Syracuse University, has a commercial in the Museum of Modern Art in NYC and since 2005 has run the first marketing company for authors - Authorbuzz.com. Rose is also the co-founder of 1001DarkNights.com and TheBlueBoxPress.com

The television series PAST LIFE, was based on Rose's novels in the Reincarnationist series.

Made in the USA
Middletown, DE
02 April 2022

63538930R00068